Elsie and
the Seal Boy

To: Eleanor and Bernadette

Elsie and the Seal Boy

Patrick O'Sullivan

WOLFHOUND PRESS

First published 1996 by
WOLFHOUND PRESS Ltd
68 Mountjoy Square
Dublin 1

Wolfhound Press receives financial assistance from the Arts Council/An Chomhairle Ealaíon, Dublin.

British Library Cataloguing in Publication Data
A catalogue record for this book is available from the British Library.

ISBN 0-86327-558-3

Cover illustration: Roslyn Davey
Cover design: Joe Gervin
Typesetting: Fingers UnLtd.
Printed in the UK by Cox & Wyman Ltd., Reading, Berks.

Chapter One

The County Kerry townland of Coonarone was a remote but beautiful place of crags and hills and fuchsia hedgerows, bright with the fire of pendulous flowers. Elsie Murphy came there to visit her aunt, Julia, one summer, little dreaming of the adventure that lay in store for her.

The coastline at Coonarone was heavily indented with little inlets and bays, some narrow and jagged at the edges, others broader and somewhat more gently curved in shape.

Elsie's aunt Julia lived alone in an old stonework farmhouse set in a sheltered nook at the base of a hill overlooking the sea. The east gable faced towards the sea and the house was fronted by an avenue, flanked on either side by a low stone wall and a row of mature cypress trees.

Julia Cronin was in her late thirties, her eyes dark, her jet black hair swept away from her forehead, her features strong but with an underlying hint of gracefulness. She had had what some of the older country people called 'a disappointment' many years before. She had been keeping company with a local man and it had been predicted that they would marry, but they had fallen out, and Julia's lover had headed for England and never returned.

Julia had only one sister, Elsie's mother, and it was the latter who had written, suggesting that Elsie might go and stay with Julia for a little while during the summer holidays. It must get lonely for Julia at times, though she would never admit it, Elsie's mother had said.

The reply from Coonarone was somewhat lukewarm. Julia professed herself to be perfectly content with her hens and her geese and her ducks, but if Elsie wished to come for a holiday she would be welcome; the clear implication was that if Elsie chose to come to Coonarone, she should not do so on the pretext of providing some company for her poor lonely spinster aunt.

When Elsie came at last to the old stonework farmhouse, however, her aunt seemed genuinely pleased to see her. Elsie looked around the huge living room. There was an enormous stone fireplace, the dresser laden with delph and a pendulum clock rhythmically beating out time on the wall. From somewhere at the back of the house, she could hear the raucous gaggling of geese and the quacking of ducks.

'The farmhouse is beautiful,' enthused Elsie.

Julia seemed pleased at her reaction to her home.

'It's much too big for one person,' Julia commented, with the merest suggestion of weariness in her tone, 'but there is no use in complaining. Too much space is better than too little.'

While they were seated at the table having a meal, Elsie observed more closely the little framed pencil sketches that stood on the mantle. They were mainly local views, the roll and swell of the sea executed from different perspectives in each of them.

'Aunt Julia, did you draw those yourself?' Elsie asked, pointing to the pictures.

'Yes, a good many years ago, but they aren't very good.' Her aunt was dismissive.

Elsie, however was genuinely impressed with them.

'Do you do any sketching now?'

'No, no. I haven't taken out my pencil and pad for years. When I was still at school, I had dreams of going to art college, but like so many other things in life, it didn't work out —'

There was an awkward silence for a few moments, as if Julia instantly regretted what she had said.

~

Elsie's bedroom was in the gable end of the house, looking out over the sea. It had an old world charm: an old oak bed and wardrobe, print curtains that had been faded by sunlight over time. Elsie stood at the window and looked out across the bay, at the brine heaving and glittering in the sun, and the fishing boats silhouetted in the distance.

'Coonarone is pleasant enough in the summertime, but in winter it is a different story,' her aunt said, looking over Elsie's shoulder. 'In winter, the bay is bleak and wild, and the breakers sweep across the rocks. By the way, there's a bicycle out in the shed. You're welcome to use it if you wish.'

Elsie smiled. She would love to go for a cycle now and then.

Knowing that Elsie was arriving, Julia had cleaned and oiled an old black bicycle that had not been ridden for years. It was not the most stylish mode of transport, but it was the thought that her aunt had taken the trouble to make it ready for her which pleased her most of all.

~

Coonarone was a beautiful place, a place far removed from the rush and bustle of city streets, a place that would never hit the headlines, but one that might grace a postcard depicting the wild and rugged grandeur of the Kerry coastline. Such were Elsie's first impressions of the environs of the farmhouse that her aunt called home.

The townland had, however, made front page news some twelve years before, and Elsie was soon to hear all about it.

'Go down to the strand and say "hello" to the "old men of the sea",' her aunt urged. 'That's what the seals are called locally. You'll see a few of them in the water near the rocks, but if you walk some distance along the strand, you'll come to a sheltered inlet where they congregate in some numbers.'

'Can I go swimming?' Elsie asked. 'I've had swimming lessons, and I promise not to stray too far from the shore. Please?'

'Okay,' Julia nodded, 'provided you keep your promise. If you don't, you will not be allowed to go swimming again,' she added firmly, suggesting that Julia was a woman whose actions would surely match her words.

Elsie mounted the old black bicycle and headed towards the sea.

~

She gasped with delight when she stood on the strand. For there they were, the old men of the sea, soft-eyed whiskery seals with their heads raised above the water. These must be the seals her aunt had told her about.

The seals seemed as curious about her as she was about them. If she was amazed at their huge streamlined bodies, they must be marvelling at her two long lower limbs as she moved about on the strand. She was tempted to put on her swimming togs at once but, no, she would walk further up the strand until she came to the inlet where her aunt had said she would find the seals massed in greater numbers.

~

Her very first day in Coonarone. It was a glorious summer's day.

She had been more than a little apprehensive as she bade her mother and her sister goodbye at the railway station, but now it seemed as if that apprehension had been unnecessary. The sunlight glinted in her soft brown eyes and added a new lustre to her rich brown hair. There were blue mussel shells strewn on the beach, and strange, strap-like seaweed cast up by the tide. But Elsie did not linger over them.

She gazed out towards the fishing boats as she strolled along. She wondered about the relationship between the fishermen and the seals. Was it a case of peaceful coexistence? Or did some of the fishermen resent the fish that were taken by the seals? Surely the numbers of fish taken were not very great. There were a good number of seals about the inlet, but she figured that the colony would be considered quite small, if measured by the size of colonies elsewhere.

The inlet seemed the perfect home for the seals, and Elsie was filled with renewed delight when she saw them, hauled out on the rocks, or swimming lethargically about in the water. She studied the inlet more closely. It was an irregular jagged V-shape, with a broken line of rocks almost like a reef at its mouth. In a few moments she had donned her swimming togs and entered the water.

A few of the seals, awkward and ungainly, slithered from their places amongst the rocks, but they seemed unperturbed by her presence. They swam about in the water as if confident of their prowess in their own environment, perhaps sensing that this newcomer had no desire to harm them.

It was only when she was in the water that Elsie began to fully appreciate the true size of the whiskery creatures about her; some of them were up to two and a half metres in length, the males or bulls much bigger in size than their female companions, the cows. The massive bulk of their elongated bodies suggested some incredible weight, though what that weight might be Elsie could not begin to imagine.

She watched their skill and agility in the water. Their bodies, despite their enormous size, were admirably adapted to their watery home. When one of them drew close to her, she saw that its fore flippers were paddle-shaped with long slender claws, an arrangement which seemed perfect for her whiskered companion. When the seal moved away, she caught a fleeting glimpse of its hind flippers. They were curiously fan-like, and they seemed to provide the propulsion as it went on its way. Elsie grinned with delight. It was as if the big grey seal were in whimsical mood, for it soon returned, curling and curving and diving about her.

What a contrast there was between the movements of the seal in the water and on land, for while the latter were often cumbersome and laboured, the former had a remarkable elegance and grace. She had never before been so close to a creature of the deep, though she had often been fascinated by seals and other sea creatures when they featured on nature programmes on television from time to time. Maybe the seal close by her was welcoming her to Coonarone. She hoped it was, for there could be no more wonderful welcome in the world.

Many of the other seals in the water were curious about her too, but they did not come as close to her as their more playful counterpart, who seemed determined to impress her with its swiftness and style. There was a strangely elemental feeling, primeval nearly, being so close to it in the water on that bright summer's day, for it was as if the seals had been in the waters off Coonarone since the first ages of the world.

Elsie stayed in the water for ages, as every time she thought of leaving it, she could almost sense the big grey seal inviting her to stay a little while longer, and a little while longer still. When she left the sea at last, she did so reluctantly.

It was only when she emerged from the water that Elsie became aware of an old fisherman sitting on a rock. He was looking out to sea, a wistful expression in his grey-green eyes. His face was lined and rugged, but there was a quiet pride and strength there too. It was a face that had known the many moods of the sea.

'I see you like the seals,' he said in a voice that was soft and lilting.

'Yes, they're brilliant!' the girl enthused, drawing nearer to him.

'They're handsome lads, to be sure,' he agreed in pensive mood. 'Did you know that some people say they aren't sea creatures at all, but people under enchantment?'

Elsie looked at him curiously. She was intrigued by this colourful revelation, and she could understand how at one time it might have been imagined that the seals had human qualities. Their whiskered heads in the water, as well as their sometimes quizzical expressions, would surely have encouraged such notions.

'Have you heard the story of the baby?' the old man went on.

Elsie shook her head.

'Well, it put Coonarone on the front page of almost every newspaper in Ireland twelve years or so ago,' he said, motioning her to sit beside him.

'You mean a true story?' Elsie intervened, for she had assumed that her companion was about to tell her some old fable again.

'As true as you and I are sitting here together,' he told her, and she could see the earnestness in his eyes. 'It all started when this young couple from up the country came to visit their relatives that lived about a mile or so further out the road,' he resumed with some relish, for he was more than pleased with the newcomer's interest. 'They had a little baby boy with them, and his mother got into the habit of coming down to the strand now and then with him. It was a very mild autumn that year, and she used to say that the fresh air was good for the child and would give him a colour.'

Elsie listened intently and longed to hear more.

'One day she took a notion to place the child on one of the ledges further up the strand while she picked a few mussels, but it seems she was in bad health and didn't she get some kind of attack. A local man found her and carried her off to the doctor but, in all the commotion, there was no thought of the child.' He paused and adjusted the peaked cap on his head. He'd heard the word which was used by some people to describe the woman's condition, but could he remember it — 'Epilepsy, yes, that was it,' he asserted with some conviction after a pause.

13

'But what happened to the baby?' Elsie asked with mounting interest.

'Well, that was the saddest part of all,' her companion told her and she could hear the regret in his tone. 'While they were bringing the mother to the doctor, the tide came in and the child was gone.'

'That's terrible,' Elsie said with genuine sadness.

'Well we searched high up and low down to try and find the baby. I was one of the searchers myself,' the old man went on. 'The unfortunate woman recovered from her attack, but she nearly lost her reason over the loss of her child and the doctor had to give her something to keep her calm. The father, the poor man, was as white as a sheet and he kept saying, "We must keep searching, we'll surely find the baby soon." But we never found hide nor hair of him.' He sighed audibly.

'And did a lot of reporters come down to Coonarone?' Elsie prompted.

'Reporters? The place was swarming with them. It was the biggest story of the autumn, — and the strangest,' her companion assured her. 'But that wasn't the end of the story, for there was an old woman in her eighties who lived back the road and she had all the *piseogs* about the seals. "That child wasn't drowned at all," she said, "but was taken by the seals. For when they saw the tide coming in, they carried him off to a safe place to rear him themselves." Some people laughed at her, of course, and said she was going a bit simple at the end of her days, but a lot of the older crowd said she mightn't be talking such foolishness at all, for wasn't it well known that seals

14

had saved human babies in the past and suckled them at their breasts.'

'Could that really be true?' Elsie asked with more than a little incredulity.

'Well now, it's not for me to say whether it's true or not,' the storyteller replied in his gentle way, 'but there was an old saying about a seal's breast milk raising an inch of fat in a week.' He paused to cast his gaze towards the seals and the water once more. 'Maybe he is out there now, the seal boy of Coonarone, and wouldn't it be a wonderful thing if he was,' he mused with such longing that Elsie found herself sharing something of the same feeling too.

~

Some time later, Elsie said goodbye to the old man and made her way back along the strand towards the spot where she had left her bicycle. She pondered over what the old man had told her. Was it possible that a baby could be reared by seals? It seemed improbable, and yet how could she be certain?

When she returned to the farmhouse, her aunt Julia told her that she had heard the story of the seal boy many times, but that's all it was, a good story.

'And there's no use wanting it to be true, for wanting doesn't change the way things are,' she added as an afterthought.

Elsie put all thoughts of the seal boy out of her mind for a little while, but they came to her again after supper. She tried to imagine what it would be like for a human, a boy, to spend all his life with the seals, to know no other friends but them, to share no other cares but theirs, to need no other love but the love that they gave him. If he existed, she would give anything in the world to meet him, but how?

Later, much later, she rose in the stillness of the night and went to the gable window that looked towards the sea. She felt strangely restless but perhaps it was just the newness of her surroundings. A full moon shone down on the calm and glassy sea. There was no wind to rustle the trees or ruffle the surface of the water. Elsie threw open the window and listened. The silence was overwhelming. Could it really be that the seal boy was out there somewhere, as the old man had suggested? Could it be that she herself might come face-to-face with him one day soon?

Chapter Two

The most notorious poacher in Coonarone was Maurice O'Connell. Maurice's father had amassed quite a lot of money in his time. He had been one of the hardest workers in the county, everyone said. Maurice's mother had doted on her only son; he could do no wrong. But now both father and mother were dead.

'After a gatherer comes a squanderer,' the saying goes, which was certainly true in this case. Maurice had always had a taste for drink, and his poaching activities had brought him to the notice of the bailiffs more than once. He had been in court several times, not only for poaching, but also at the behest of creditors whose bills had gone unpaid. Eventually, his father's farm was sold, and all that remained of Maurice's inheritance was a modest bungalow and a marshy field some distance from the bungalow.

Maurice often boasted of the great plans he had, but most of his grand schemes came to nothing. He knew that people laughed at him behind his back, and he deeply resented this.

'I'll show them. I'll show them all,' Maurice said to himself, for now he had a new scheme. In fact, it had become almost an obsession with him.

~

The new scheme arose from a documentary he had heard on the radio about smuggling along the coast of Kerry in the eighteenth century. He was about to switch the radio off, when he heard Coonarone mentioned, and his ears perked up.

Apparently, in 1699, the British Parliament passed an Act which, in effect, prohibited the export of wool or woollen goods. By the year 1730, the price of wool in Ireland ranged between five pence and twelve pence a pound. In France, wool fetched from two shillings and six pence for plain wool up to six shillings for combed wool. Naturally, it came to pass that wool was regularly smuggled to France, with large quantities of brandy, wine, tea and tobacco being illegally imported on the return voyages.

According to the radio programme, though there had been some smuggling along the coast at Coonarone, the area had been more celebrated for another activity: the wrecking of ships.

The Wreckers of Coonarone, like their counterparts the world over, lured passing ships onto the rocks in bad weather by deceiving them with false lights. The wrecking of the *Ellen Maria* in 1752 was the most infamous of them all. The handsome sloop had foundered on the rocks and, whereas most ships had been forgotten, the *Ellen Maria* continued to capture the imagination of the locals. Legend had it that she had carried treasure on board.

Though Maurice had heard versions of the story of the *Ellen Maria* a great many times before, it was the radio programme that brought it into sharp focus once more. He vowed, there and then, that he would get his hands on that treasure if it was the last thing he'd do.

~

One fine morning when Maurice came to check the nets that he had set, he was less than pleased to find that the seals had eaten great chunks of some of the salmon trapped in them.

'Those bloody seals,' he muttered dourly. 'If I had my way, I'd shoot the bloody lot of them, no matter what anyone said.'

As he set the engine in motion once more and headed back to the shore, Maurice was in thoughtful mood.

'If I'm to find that treasure, I'll need an accomplice.' But who? Who could he trust?

~

Elsie came daily to swim with the seals. Her sense of wonder at them increased rather than diminished each time she saw them. One particular big grey seal had become her special friend. Now, when he came

19

close to her, she could see the strong hind flippers that provided his propulsion. The big grey pushed himself along, one webbed flipper fully flexed, the other relaxed awaiting its turn. The seals were perfectly adapted to their watery habitat, smooth, sleek and stream-lined.

One overcast morning, Julia came down to the beach to watch her swim. The water was surprisingly warm and Elsie splashed around contentedly for some time, until Julia reminded her that it was time for lunch.

'It's a pity they don't give birth till October or November,' Elsie said with some regret as she left the water. 'I'd love to see the little pups. They're born on land, aren't they?'

'Yes, the mothers come ashore before giving birth,' her aunt replied, 'but they use a special inlet for the pupping season. I love to come down and watch the pups. They're little dotes, covered with soft white fur. You'd be tempted to pick one of them up and take them home.'

'Are the mothers very protective?' Elsie inquired.

'Oh yes. They become very aggressive if any other seal comes too close, or if there are seagulls flying around,' her aunt told her. 'And there are always seagulls when a pup is born, squabbling over the afterbirth.'

'Ugh,' Elsie grimaced. This image did not appeal to her in the least.

'Do you know, a grey seal pup drinks up to two and a half litres of milk a day,' her aunt continued. 'Is it any wonder the little pups begin to look like furry barrels in a matter of days. But the poor mothers lose an awful lot of weight. They don't get to feed at all while suckling their young, which can last three to four weeks.'

'I suppose they feed as much as they can during the summer months and build up their reserves of fat?' Elsie speculated.

'They must do,' Julia agreed, smiling. 'But you should hear the cries the pups make when they're hungry. They sound just like human babies.'

Elsie stood a moment and thought.

'Maybe that's why people think the seals saved the little baby from drowning and reared it themselves?' she suggested with ever-increasing fascination.

Julia did not contradict her.

'If the seal boy really does exist,' Elsie went on, 'you'd think there would have been some sightings of him, especially in recent years as he grew older.'

'Oh, plenty of people will tell you they think they caught a glimpse of him at one time or another,' Julia told her, 'but if you ask them what he looked like, they'll tell you it all happened so quickly they really can't be sure.'

Elsie frowned. This was a disappointment.

'Over a year ago,' her aunt went on, 'Paul Sheehan took photographs down here, one wild winter's day, and in one of them, there's an outline that he thinks could be that of a boy running along the strand.'

Elsie's spirits rose again.

'Who is Paul Sheehan? Does he live near here? Could I meet him and see the photograph?' she bubbled excitedly.

'Paul is in college, studying to be a vet. He should be home on holidays at the moment. I'm sure he wouldn't mind showing you.'

~

At that very moment, Paul was dismounting from his shiny black motorcycle, and approaching a rusted gate. Paul was in his early twenties, with neatly groomed jet black hair and sporting an earring in one ear. He stood at the gate and fixed his gaze on a piebald horse in the field. It was obvious that the owner either didn't know the first thing about horses, or didn't care. The poor horse was in very bad condition. Its hooves needed to be trimmed. It hadn't been groomed in months. The horse was struggling to find a few meagre mouthfuls of grass in the already well-cropped field.

Paul's pensive mood was broken by the approach of an old battered yellow van down the road, smoke spewing from its rickety exhaust pipe. The driver was the owner of both the field and the horse, Maurice O'Connell.

'What business have you to be standing at my gate?' he demanded as he emerged from the van.

'That mare you bought from the Travellers at Puck Fair last year, she's not the picture of health, is she?' Paul observed bluntly, though he suspected that his comments would irk Maurice.

'Well, is that a fact now?' Maurice countered cynically. 'And isn't it well for you, with your motorbike and your leather jacket and your earring, with nothing better to do than find fault with another's property.'

'Can't you see she's little better than skin and bone?' Paul persisted, for he did not mind being insulted if Maurice was prompted to do something about the horse. 'And she must be in pain walking about when her hooves are that long.'

'Clear off out of my sight, Sheehan, or you'll be in pain before you know it,' Maurice retorted with sudden vengefulness. 'I'm not one of your father's toadies, and don't you forget it!'

'What's my father got to do with it?' Paul asked, bewildered.

'A pillar of society, a man of the people, that's your father. Mr Councillor Sheehan, sir,' Maurice sneered. 'I went to him, cap in hand, a few years back, to see would he help me get a grant to build a small trawler, but I might as well have been whistling in the wind.' He arched his eyebrows in disgust and paused to light a cigarette.

'I'm sure he did his best for you, like he does for everyone,' Paul countered. 'But even if you've got some kind of grudge against my father, or me, that's no reason to let the horse suffer.'

'Clear off out of here,' Maurice snapped. 'When did you or your sort ever lift a finger to help the likes of me? When did you or your father, with your fine shop in the village and your big house, ever know a poor day?'

Paul sighed with frustration. There seemed to be very little hope of making Maurice see sense. He would even have offered to take a look at the horse himself and have her hooves trimmed at his own expense, if he thought it would do any good. He returned to his motorcycle, put his helmet on and rode away, Maurice eyeing him balefully.

~

The Sheehans lived in a large modern house about half a mile from the village and, later that afternoon, Elsie walked up the driveway to the door. She'd left her bicycle near the gate. The house was in total contrast to the old stonework farmhouse where her aunt lived. It was garishly white and angular, its lines hard and cold, with big aluminium window frames glinting in the sunlight. The manicured lawns offered little comfort, for there was not a single shrub or flower in sight. It was all too clinical.

A young man answered the door.

'Excuse me, I'm l-looking for Paul Sheehan?' she stuttered, suddenly nervous.

'That's me,' he replied cheerfully.

She explained why she had called, getting more confident by the minute. Paul invited her in and ushered her into the sitting room.

She liked Paul the moment she met him. He was pleasant and smiling, and interested in her impressions of Coonarone.

He left her briefly, returning with a glass of orange and some cake, and then went off again to find the photograph.

It was some minutes before he returned, armed with several folders of photographs.

'I invented a kind of filing system of my own. Sometimes it doesn't work,' he admitted with a good-natured laugh.

Elsie placed her glass to one side as he began to pass photographs to her, one by one.

'They were all taken one wild day in November. They're not quite the stuff postcards are made of,' Paul remarked ruefully, 'but you can see some of the white seal pups there.'

He went on to explain that he'd taken some of the earlier photographs from the shore, but then decided to go out in his boat to vary the shots.

'The rain was pelting down in icy sheets, and visibility was very poor. I was probably mad to put to sea in those conditions. Anyway, I was clicking away with my camera when suddenly I thought I saw something dash along the shore.' He paused briefly. 'I was so surprised that, instead of pressing the shutter again and again, I just sat with my mouth open. You see, the strand had been totally deserted. Only a madman like me would be out in such weather.' He grinned at her. Then he handed the most intriguing photograph of all to Elsie and added, 'It was almost too late when I thought of the camera.'

Elsie studied it carefully. Jagged grey cliffs in the background, the seals on the strand, the rough sea, and a blurred shape at the water's edge. It could indeed be a boy running along the beach, but the image was so unclear that it might be anything. Even if it was a boy, who could say that it was the seal boy? It could have been any of the local boys.

Paul seemed to read her mind.

'As soon as I developed the photographs, I got really curious. I then checked around to see if any of the local schoolboys had been on the beach that day. I drew a complete blank. Somehow *The Kerryman* got wind of the word and decided to run a story on it. The editor was a bit reluctant to publish the photograph at first, as he wasn't sure if it was a fake or genuine. It's so easy to fake photographs these days. People have done it more than once with UFOs and the like.'

'And how did they satisfy themselves that it was genuine?' Elsie prompted.

'They gave it to some scientist, an expert in photography,' Paul explained. 'When he had carried out his various tests, he concluded that the photograph was not a fake. But he came to another more interesting conclusion too.'

Elsie waited patiently.

'He said it was highly unlikely to be a trick of the light; that it was almost certainly an object moving at great speed, which is what I believed I'd seen.'

Paul was delighted with Elsie's interest in the photograph and the story of the seal boy. So many people had so little imagination these days. They tended to be dismissive about such things.

Elsie was more than pleased with her visit too. The photograph itself might not prove or disprove anything, but if someone like Paul believed in the possibility of the seal boy, then her hopes of coming face-to-face with him one day might not be so far-fetched after all.

Could it have been the seal boy? Why was he running so fast along the strand? Was he rushing to one of the seals in labour, in distress? It was a plausible theory. But was it based on fact or fantasy?

Elsie bid Paul goodbye.

'If you like, you could come out in the boat some time with me,' Paul suggested and Elsie agreed eagerly.

As she cycled home, turning things over in her mind, she took little note of the battered yellow van coming towards her. Maurice, the driver of the van, was also lost in thought. His thoughts were not of the seal boy, however, but on the long lost treasure of the *Ellen Maria*. He had thought long and hard about a suitable partner for this daring enterprise, and had hit upon a prospective candidate at last. He was on his way to see him now.

Chapter Three

Julia had a visitor, an English man called Malcolm Harold, and he came to the farmhouse more than once over the next few days. He had rented an old-fashioned cottage and planned to stay in Coonarone for at least a few weeks. He was researching a book about coastal communities in Britain and Ireland, and how they had evolved down through the years. He had come to Coonarone to find out more about the smuggling trade in the eighteenth century and was anxious to hear about the wrecking of the *Ellen Maria*. Someone had recommended that he visit Julia because she was interested in local history and knew 'a great deal about that sort of thing'.

Malcolm Harold was a pleasant, affable, but sometimes serious man in his late thirties. His hair, greying at the temples, and his silver-rimmed spectacles gave him something of an intellectual mien, as did his fondness for thirties-style v-necked jumpers and tweed caps.

When Elsie arrived home, she was invited to join Julia and Mr Harold. She sat quietly, unobtrusively. This was the first time that Elsie heard anything about Coonarone's smuggling past. Apparently Julia had spent some time working in the great house of Coonarone as 'a general dogsbody', as she put it, for Miss Victoria King, the gracious old lady who now owned it. Miss King's ancestors were heavily involved in the smuggling trade and one of their number had been the leader of the notorious wreckers.

'Maybe we could visit her. I'll telephone Miss King, tell her about your interest, Mr Harold, and see could we arrange to call to talk to her,' Julia said.

'Can I come too?' Elsie pleaded. 'I would love to see the big house.'

Julia nodded. 'Of course you can.'

~

A few days later, on a bright morning in mid-July, with the delicious perfume of summer roses filling the air, Elsie, Julia and the Englishman stood amid the faded elegance of the great hall of the ancestral home of the Kings. Miss King kept her silvery hair in place beneath a discreet hair net. She wore a tailored blue costume that echoed the colour of her eyes. She spoke with a cultured Anglo-Irish accent that Elsie found somewhat intimidating at first.

'Oh yes, not a few upper class families in Kerry plied the smuggling trade in those days,' she assured them, as she led the way towards the room that had served as her father's study. 'The gentry felt quite aggrieved in those days about the restrictions placed on the export of Irish wool, but surely you know that already, Mr Harold.'

Elsie looked about her with delight; the grandeur of the plasterwork ceilings overhead, the shining oak boards underfoot.

'My father was very interested in things of the sea,' Miss King said, explaining why so much of the material relating to the naval exploits of the family had found its way into his study.

The study was a rather gloomy room, with dark brown velvet drapes on the windows. Oak bookcases lined the walls, their shelves laden with musty tomes. There was a plain writing table and a few leather-backed armchairs. However, the room was dominated by a huge portrait of a woman in period dress which hung above the mantle. She had long dark hair, and deep dark eyes, eyes that were cold, severe and ruthless.

'Black Annie. That's what they called her,' Miss King offered. 'As you've no doubt heard, Mr Harold, some of the exploits of my ancestors were less than savoury.' Her voice took on a note of quiet pride. Though she may not approve of the activities of the wreckers, she seemed relieved that at least some of the women of the family had been noted for something more than small talk and lace-making.

'Do you know how they set about wrecking the ships, my dear?' she asked, turning to Elsie.

With some embarrassment, Elsie admitted that she didn't.

'Well, when the victims' sail was seen far off on a stormy night, the wreckers turned out a horse or two to graze in a field on the cliff top,' Miss King explained. 'They tied a lantern about the horse's neck and, viewed from a distance, the lantern light seemed to rise and fall, like that of a ship in the distance. In this way, the sailors were fooled into believing that there was open water before them, with a ship ahead. Then they made straight for the rocks and did not discover their mistake until it was far too late.'

Elsie grimaced. The practice seemed quite brutal. She was relieved to hear that such deliberate wreckings had not been as widespread along the Kerry coastline as elsewhere.

'Miss King, could you tell me why the wrecking of the *Ellen Maria* was so special?' the Englishman asked in his soft-spoken way.

'I suppose it was special because there was one survivor,' Miss King answered. 'Generally there were no survivors. The wreckers saw to that. But somehow the captain of the *Ellen Maria* managed to escape the slaughter and was not discovered for a day or so when at last he was found half-drowned and half-naked in one of the inlets.'

'And how come he was allowed to live to tell the tale?' Mr Harold persisted.

'He would have been put to death at once by those who found him, had they not searched him and come upon some documents, amongst them the one that saved him,' Miss King replied.

The tick of the mantle clock was loud and measured in the stillness of the room.

'The one describing the treasure on board the ship?' Elsie's aunt suddenly realised.

'Yes, the document gave details of a chest full of French silverware, magnificent pieces,' Miss King went on.

Elsie listened, gazing intently at the granite face in the portrait.

'The captain was brought up here to the old house, the one that stood on this site before the present house was built. On the instructions of Black Annie, he was given every care.'

'Did she hope that when he recovered he would tell her where he had hidden the silver, because she suspected him of carrying it off and hiding it?' Mr Harold speculated.

The hostess nodded and continued. 'Well, the captain did recover, but he was more than reluctant to share his secret with anyone, and if he had hidden it in one of the caves, the wreckers might never find it. The cliffs in these parts are riddled with caves.'

This last revelation fascinated Elsie most of all for, if the caves had concealed the secret of the French silver for over two centuries, might they not also have concealed the secret of the seal boy for a mere twelve years?

'The days became weeks and the weeks became months and, not surprisingly, some of Black Annie's accomplices began to lose all patience with their prisoner,' Miss King resumed after a pause. 'But that was when the story took an unexpected twist, for Black Annie had fallen in love with the captain. She insisted that the wreckers be patient with him, give him time, and, just to keep her cronies happy, she promised faithfully that she would inveigle his secret out of him in time. The captain did not return Black Annie's love, however, and remained stubborn to the last, though she told him that she was the only reason he was still alive.' Miss King was now drawing near the end of her story.

'The men became more and more aggressive and vindictive, but still she overruled any suggestion of harming the captain. One night, however, when she wasn't home, he was bundled out of the house and murdered on the strand. Black Annie was furious to the point of distraction. They had been such utter fools, she said. They had killed the captain and his secret died with him.'

'Was she really in love with him, or did she just want to get her hands on the silver?' Julia asked, the merest hint of cynicism in her tone.

'Oh, you may be sure all that interested her at first was the silver,' Miss King agreed, 'but love is a strange thing. She must have been in love with him to protect him so fiercely against his would-be aggressors. She wasn't generally known for her sentimentality. Maybe she hoped she could have the best of both worlds; that he would fall in love with her *and* tell her his secret too.'

The story finished, the little group wandered around the study, Mr Harold being especially fascinated with the rows and rows of books that no one had read for years.

'Did the document describing the silver survive?' he wondered aloud.

'Yes, but I haven't seen it for years. My father became quite forgetful and confused in his old age. If you'd care to come back another day, you may take as long as you like to look through the books and drawers in the study. You might find the document, if you're lucky.'

Mr Harold looked around him. He'd need to be very lucky to find it.

~

Later that afternoon, Elsie swam with the seals again, the sun twinkling on the water. The big grey seal that had become her special favourite was as playful as ever. That was why she had named him Sugra. The water had an emerald tinge and, though the seals hauled out on the rocks appeared a bit startled at first by her coming, there was no mad panic to get into the water. It was as if they were beginning to accept her coming amongst them as a matter of no great consequence, which pleased her very much. There seemed to be about twenty to twenty-five seals, on the rocks and in the water, but Julia had assured her that their numbers were much greater during the breeding season. Many of them must head off elsewhere when the breeding season was over, perhaps out to sea to feed, while those that remained behind moved down from the breeding site to the craggy inlet that was their favourite haunt during the summer. It was as if they reserved the breeding site just for that purpose, and the group that chose to stay on made a point of moving some distance from it.

Now a bull plunged into the water off the rocks and dived through the shimmering green, silvery bubbles winking in his fur. Sugra swam lazily about her, but soon the other big grey became the focus of her attention. It was fabulous to see how skilfully and gracefully he, like Sugra, manoeuvred the great mass of his body, curving and fluid. Down and down he dived, deeper and deeper still. The seconds ticked by and he did not reappear. A minute passed, two minutes, three, four and then he rose to the surface once more. Elsie was envious of this feat. A human diver would have to fit a big cumbersome tank of gas on his back to do the same thing. Although seals are mammals and have to breathe air, the big grey seal must have enormous reserves of oxygen to enable it to stay underwater for so long.

About twenty minutes later, Elsie joined her new friend Paul on his boat. He wanted to take some more photographs, and had invited Elsie to come along. Elsie had never seen the sea so beautifully green before, emerald green. She told Paul about the big grey's diving prowess and he was able to explain it.

'I read somewhere that seals not only store oxygen in their blood, but also in their muscles. Not only that, do you know their heart beat changes when they dive? It's about forty beats per minute when they're under water, but as soon as they surface, it shoots up to one hundred and twenty beats per minute.'

'But how does that help them?' Elsie asked, bemused.

'It speeds up their respiration once they surface, to get rid of the waste carbon dioxide in double-quick time and take in more oxygen.'

'So that's why they can dive again and again once they have a breather at the surface. I wish I could do that,' she added wistfully.

Elsie moved her gaze towards the entrances to the caves in the cliffs. Paul stopped the boat to click the shutter of his camera.

'Each entrance gives access to a network of caves,' Paul told her. 'It's quite easy to lose your way in them or get trapped by the incoming tide. There have been a few near misses when foolhardy tourists have gone to explore them alone. Apparently, there are some caves there that the seawater no longer reaches, set deep in the cliffs. And don't ask me to explain that, because I can't,' Paul added with a laugh. Elsie grinned.

It was not long before the boat was directly opposite the inlet used by the seals for breeding, and Elsie was delighted when Paul suggested they might go ashore and have a look around. Elsie mentioned the seal boy again as they walked along the strand. Suddenly Paul remembered something that might, like the photograph, lead one to believe that he really did exist, if one were that way inclined.

'It was the vet in the village that told me about it,' he explained when Elsie begged him to tell her more. 'He came to see the pups last October twelve months or so. It's wrong to disturb them too much during the breeding season, but he came alone.'

'And what happened?' Elsie prompted as the two of them clambered across some rocky crags.

'Well, he noticed one of the pups with an ugly red weal in its side and though he was tempted to help it, he decided it was best to let nature take its course,' Paul went on. 'After all, baby greys may look soft and cuddly, but if you get too close, they don't think twice about sinking their teeth in your hand. I suppose they can't be blamed if they think they're being threatened.' He paused to look at two seagulls soaring gracefully overhead.

Elsie followed his gaze, and grimaced as she remembered what her aunt had told her about the greedy gulls squabbling over the membranes after the birth of the pups.

'Even though he gave no help, he was anxious to try and monitor the pup's progress; that would be virtually impossible when all the pups had been born, but it was still quite early in the season,' Paul continued, genuinely pleased that he had found someone who shared his interest. 'When the vet came back the second time, he noticed something very curious. Someone appeared to have applied a square of damp cloth to the wound. He couldn't investigate how it stayed in place, but it did, even when the furry pup scurried off.'

'That's strange,' Elsie said, more intrigued than ever, 'but maybe one of the locals had been moved by the little fellow's plight and had taken a risk to try and help him.'

'Someone untrained would come away with a very bloody hand if they tried anything so foolish,' her companion reminded her, 'and the vet did take the trouble to enquire if any unusual hand wounds had been reported, but there were none.' He stopped, puzzled. 'It's possible that the cloth covered the wound quite by accident, but that seems too much like coincidence.'

'But where would the seal boy get cloth?' Elsie persisted.

'There are always things washed in by the tide, especially high tides in winter, so that would be possible.'

Maybe, just maybe, the seal boy was not a figment of her imagination after all, Elsie mused, as Paul began to show her how to use his camera.

~

Maurice had found himself a partner who would help him search for the hoard of French silver that had become part of the folklore of the townland of Coonarone. This was Toby Burke, who generally attributed his lack of progress in life to what he called 'a run of bad luck'. His wife often nagged him for 'giving in to Maurice and his daft schemes,' as she put it, and though Maurice promised faithfully that on this occasion he would keep his plans to himself, it wasn't long before he was making idle boasts that the treasure would soon be his, much to the hapless Toby's annoyance.

'I'll blow their heads off if they've taken another one of my salmon,' Maurice vowed vindictively as he and Toby travelled out in his boat to examine their nets next morning.

Elsie had risen early and made her way down to the strand. It looked like it was going to be another beautiful day. She watched the poachers at work, keeping out of sight.

Suddenly her heart missed a beat. Maurice pulled in a salmon that had been mutilated by the seals and next moment he grabbed his rifle. He fixed the sights on a big grey bull hauled out on a rock. Elsie gulped in horror.

'Let them stew in their own blood for a while, maybe they'll clear off then,' Maurice muttered grimly as he prepared to pull the trigger, the other man watching him with nervous apprehension. Toby wished his partner wasn't so fiery and quick-tempered. The seals hadn't done that much damage and, after all, they had a right to be there too.

Elsie held her breath. The air was still and tense. She waited, frozen, for the shot to explode and rip the stillness asunder. Maurice grinned with malevolent delight.

'Hold it there, me little beauty,' he said as he held the sight of the gun fixed fast on the enormous body of the seal. He savoured this moment of power, a kind of blood lust coursing through him until his finger itched.

At last, Elsie found her voice and was just about to scream out, to shout 'STOP!', when suddenly the boat tilted to one side. The gun fell from Maurice's grasp as he was flung into the water.

Chapter Four

Maurice had been furious with his partner, accusing him of moving about and unbalancing the boat, though Toby swore on his oath that he had not moved at all. To make matters worse, Maurice's gun had plummeted to the depths and could not be retrieved.

Elsie watched the drama intently and, though she had not seen Toby move, what else could have caused the boat to tilt so abruptly? Could it have been the seal boy come to protect the seals? It was an intriguing thought.

~

Two days later, Mr Harold came to the old stonework farmhouse with some exciting news. He had found the document describing the silver on board the *Ellen*

Maria in the study at the big house and Miss King had allowed him to borrow it, to have it photographed and photocopied. It would make a wonderful illustration for his book.

Now he spread out the yellowed parchment on the big wooden table in the kitchen. Elsie's heart drummed with anticipation. The details about the silver were written in an elegant script in fading black ink.

'It would have been a fine haul,' Malcolm enthused with unconcealed joy. 'Two-handled cups with covers, elaborate candlesticks, soup tureens and sauce boats, wine fountains, cisterns and ewers, a centre-piece called an epergne, tea pots, coffee pots and chocolate pots, sugar bowls and cream jugs.'

Elsie's eyes shone with delight. The list described an Aladdin's cave of silverware.

'And look here,' Malcolm went on with unbridled enthusiasm. 'It describes the decoration on some of the pieces in detail: grotesque masks, nymphs and satyrs, birds and beasts and butterflies, shells and scallops and tritons. Isn't it amazing that the wreckers chose to wreck a ship with such a fantastic cargo in its hold, rather than capture it.'

'Maybe they had no idea of what was on board,' Julia interjected. 'Anyway, even though the document claims to describe the silver carried by the *Ellen Maria*, who's to say that it was ever placed on board? Or that the ship did not pull into some port and the silver brought ashore before the wrecking at Coonarone?'

'Anything is possible,' Malcolm admitted, though he seemed unwilling to allow his high spirits to be dampened too much by the other's caution, for it seemed to him that the most likely probability was that the silver had still been on board at the time of the wrecking. After all, Black Annie had been a very astute woman. If she hadn't been convinced that the silver was still somewhere close by, she would never have allowed the captain to live long enough to fall in love with him.

When he had the document photographed and photocopied, the next step would be to try and pinpoint exactly where the *Ellen Maria* had gone down. Nobody seemed too sure and there were, in fact, several conflicting theories on the matter.

After he had carefully folded away the document, he noticed something different about Julia.

'Have you changed your hair?'

Julia blushed.

'I had it cut.'

She had had it cut but, instead of sweeping it back from her forehead, she now had it arranged more loosely, which softened her face and made her seem less severe, though not diminishing in the least the quiet strength that was such a facet of her features.

'It suits you. Sorry I didn't notice it before, I was just so engrossed in the document.'

Julia blushed even more, and muttered something about planning to do something with her hair for ages. It was as if she wanted the subject changed, and quickly.

'You really must get out your pencil and sketch pad,' Malcolm suggested.

Julia seemed much more receptive to the idea than she had been when Elsie had proposed it on the first day of her visit to the farmhouse.

'You've got a natural gift for sketching and it's a shame to waste it. Besides, I really would like to use some of your sketches in the chapter on Coonarone.'

'Please do, Aunt Julia, please, please do,' Elsie pleaded.

'There now, it's unanimous,' Malcolm grinned. 'Both Elsie and I would like to see you sketch again.'

'Well if that's the way of it, I suppose I can't say no,' Julia smiled.

~

The sky was overcast and gloomy, the weather forecast spoke of gales on the way sometime later. This did not deter Elsie from swimming with Sugra however, though the water felt cold, much colder, and she shivered when she entered it. Sugra came towards her as if to welcome her and it was such a wonderful feeling to be welcomed by this big sleek creature of the wild. It was that afternoon that Elsie saw him capture a fish for the very first time.

The seals, like humans, seemed to be opportunists, they ate whatever came their way. That was why they sometimes preyed upon the luckless salmon trapped in the nets illegally set by Maurice and his accomplice. But they were quite capable of catching their own fish too, as Sugra so expertly demonstrated. One moment he seemed quite relaxed and playful, next moment he sprang into action when a foolish flounder strayed across his path. His turn of speed was incredible for, in a split second he was upon the flounder, thrusting his neck forward and snapping at it with his jaws. The flounder disappeared in one swift gulp and though

Elsie felt sorry for it, she marvelled again at Sugra's skill.

Soon the atmosphere became drowsy and lethargic, the sky still and tense. Was this the calm before a storm? Elsie's aunt had assured her that summer gales were not uncommon along this part of the coast.

The seals had another skill which intrigued Elsie: they sometimes slept in the water. They were said to be 'bottling' when they indulged in this sea-sleeping. Paul had told her about it and now she grinned with pleasure when she saw a few of them remain perfectly motionless, their whiskered heads held upright above the water. This was one of their most endearing qualities, Elsie told herself. Before she had come to Coonarone she had seen seals featured on nature programmes on television and, though she had been interested in them, she tended to regard them as one great cumbersome mass of ungainly blubber struggling about on great craggy rocks, dripping and dark with the wash of the spray.

Now, however, she realised that there was much more to seals than she had ever imagined and, just like humans, many of them seemed to have their own quirks and eccentricities too. It was all too easy to be dismissive of them but the more she understood them, the more she admired them.

There was always a barrier between herself and Sugra. She could never get close enough to stroke him or hug him. He appeared to resent such overtures and responded accordingly, but that was very much part of his innate wildness and it added to the aura of mystique that surrounded him.

Elsie played about a bit more but, realising that a nasty storm was on its way, she reluctantly left the sea and headed for home.

~

The gales did come later that evening, battering the coastline with unfettered passion, great sheets of rain slanting in from the sea and seagulls screaming in the heavens. The waves were whipped high against the rocks, great foaming crests of spray curling all around. The seals were nowhere to be seen. Perhaps they had sought refuge in their familiar caves.

Maurice struggled to drag his boat towards the upper reaches of the strand where it might be safe, out of danger's way. He strained his eyes across the water. His nets were still in place. It would be a great loss if they were washed away but it would be too risky to try and pull them in now. The wind was at his back and he was blown towards his battered yellow van, struggling to keep his oilskin cap in place.

~

The solitary wiper wobbled back and forth on the right hand side of the windscreen, barely coping with the rain flooding relentlessly down.

Toby, despite his apparent fecklessness in many other departments, was an avid reader and was confident that he had seen prints of maps in a local history book published in the Seventies. He had promised to try and find some old maps of Coonarone in the library. However, Maurice had little faith in him.

Toby is so unreliable, he told himself.

Maurice had scarcely made his way indoors, however, and set the frying pan on the cooker when the disgruntled Toby arrived, book in hand.

'I wonder why I bother,' Toby said, 'when you go and broadcast our plans to half the county.'

Maurice plonked two plates of greasy sausages and fried eggs on the table.

'Give it here,' Maurice demanded impatiently. He flicked though the pages, in the manner of an expert in map reading. 'Have you looked through the book already, Toby? Did it make any mention of the wrecking and the silver?'

'Yeah, I looked through it all right,' Toby assured him, 'but it isn't much help.'

The author of the book had written that it was simply not known where exactly along the coastline of Coonarone the wrecking had taken place, nor was it known if the wreckers had confined their activities to one particularly treacherous stretch of water where rocks abounded, or if they had been less than fussy, luring their victims to whatever stretch they could, since most of the coastline was rocky anyway. But the writer did offer some pointers to possible locations where wrecking might have taken place.

'Well? And —?' Maurice prompted impatiently as he stuffed his mouth with food.

'He lists some of the old names for individual rocks and clusters of rocks,' Toby explained. 'There's a cluster called *Carraigeacha na Fola*, the Rocks of Blood, which could be where the wreckings took place. There's one called *Carraig a' Bhriseadh*, the Breaking Rock, and another cluster called *Leaba na Fhomhoracha*, the Pirates' Bed.'

He pointed to the relevant places on the map but his companion did not seem unduly impressed.

'Look, Maurice, if you think we're going to find a map with the spot marked "X" like they do in the films, you can forget it.'

He paused to pour himself a mug of tea.

'It narrows things down a bit anyway,' he resumed. 'We can start by searching the caves in the vicinity of these rocks and that should keep us busy for quite a while.'

~

Elsie stood at her bedroom window in the farmhouse. The sea had such a different aspect now. The waves that had lapped gently at her feet were swept furiously over the rocks, great fountains of spray rising and falling all around. Her aunt and the Englishman were down in the living room talking about the wreckings, but Elsie had sensed that they wanted to be alone.

Mr Harold had been telling them about the types of ships used by the smugglers in the eighteenth century.

'The *Ellen Maria* was a sloop, with rigging fore and aft. But the smugglers used sleek-hulled cutters which were similar to sloops in many ways.'

Now Elsie tried to imagine what the scene must have been like when a majestic sailing ship foundered on the rocks off Coonarone in weather such as this, the rocks tearing through the hull, the wild grey waves seething with fury and pouring in, the towering mast creaking and groaning and at last brought low as the proud ship tumbled sideways, the sails in tatters, streaming in the wind, the sailors struggling in the water and the wreckers rushing from the shore to claim their grim plunder.

~

The winds had abated next morning and the sky was awash with silvery light when Paul rode his motorcycle along the coast road. He rode at some speed, for someone had come to tell him they had seen Maurice's piebald mare in some distress in her field. When he came to the field, he clambered over the rusted gate and dashed to the horse's side.

The mare was lying on the ground, shivering and trembling, and Paul cringed with disgust when he saw her. She was clearly malnourished. He could count her ribs and the rain and the wind had brought on a sudden fever. He draped her gently with an old blanket he had brought with him. At least that would keep her warm for a little while, but he would have to do more this time. He couldn't let the unfortunate horse suffer any longer. Soon he was on his motorcycle again.

He called to one of the neighbours and asked him to fetch the poor animal in his horsebox and bring her to Paul's home. There was a barn there, where he could give her some nourishment, have her hooves trimmed and treat her until she recovered. Maurice could say what he liked, he had had more than enough time to do something for the mare and he had not done so.

~

About half an hour later, Maurice was on his way to check his nets. It would be a miracle if they were still in place.

As he passed his field, he could scarcely believe his eyes. There was that git Paul and one of his lackeys loading his horse into a horsebox.

'What the bloody hell do you thing you're doing, Sheehan?' he demanded angrily as he struggled across the rain sodden field. 'Get that horse out of that horsebox this instant or I'll have you up before the judge for thieving and a lot more besides.'

'You won't have me up before the judge and you know it,' Paul countered with conviction, for if there was anything which maddened him, it was mindless cruelty to animals. 'You're not fit to look after the horse and, if you stop me taking her now, I'll have the ISPCA on your back before you know it.'

The owner of the horsebox sat in his car in stony silence, fearful that Maurice might suddenly vent his anger on him too.

'Oh, I'm not fit to look after her, Mr Sheehan, am I not? And if you had your way, you'd trample me and my kind into the gutter.'

'Don't change the subject, Maurice, you were always very good at blaming someone else, but you won't get off the hook that easily this time,' Paul assured him with a firmness that surprised him, for there were many in the townland of Coonarone who steered clear of Maurice and his fiery temperament.

'How dare you lecture me, you snivelling little upstart!' Maurice screamed in a voice calculated to intimidate.

When Paul turned to walk away, Maurice flung himself upon him. They grappled with one another, punching and kicking with a grimness and resolve that startled the driver of the car, though it did not even enter his head that he should try to separate them.

Let them have at it and may the best man win, the driver thought.

Maurice's face was a grimace of rage, his features distorted with rancour and resentment. He had taken the arrogance and condescension of all the petty little nobodies like the Sheehans for far too long.

His strong bony fists thudded again and again against Paul's chest. Maurice was taken aback at the power of the other's punches when they hit home. He shouldn't really have been surprised, however, for Paul trained with the university rowing club which developed his muscles and strengthened his forearms.

Paul saw the contest as a struggle to decide the fate of a poor ill-used horse, but for his adversary it was much more. It was a matter of injured pride and honour and getting one up on the leeches who always seemed determined to belittle him and keep him down.

They gasped and panted and fell to the ground, Maurice struggling to claw his opponent's face with his right hand. They rolled on the muddy rain-drenched grass. Still they punched and kicked and Paul could see the malice in the other's eyes. But he would not yield. For the sake of the horse he would not give way. As the fight progressed, their punches grew wilder, more reckless and largely ineffectual.

In the end, Maurice struggled to rise to his feet, staggered backwards and fell motionless to the ground, dazed and exhausted. Paul rose slowly, wiped the blood from his lower lip and made his way painfully to the car.

~

After the storm had waned, Elsie wandered back down to the strand. Seaweed and driftwood and bits of rubbish were scattered here and there, washed up by the tide. The seals had returned and they seemed relieved that the gales had passed and gone. Sugra was not amongst them but Elsie was not unduly perturbed. He often went missing for a few hours at a time. He valued his freedom and she did not wish to deprive him of it in the slightest. After all, though he might be her friend, he was still a wild creature, not a pet. A strange fanciful thought entered her head. What if she come upon a piece of the old French silverware washed ashore by the storms?

Minutes later, she did make a curious discovery, but it was not the brilliant sheen of silver that caught her eye. Rather it was a strange entanglement of various kinds of seaweed, suspended from a long brown ribbon of laminaria. It was as if the seaweed had been woven and meshed together before being hung from the strand of laminaria, which might easily have served the function of a belt, and a strong leathery belt at that.

Elsie's heart began to pound again and her brown eyes shone with anticipation. A hoard of antique French silver would surely be a marvellous find, but she would give all the French silver in the world to come face-to-face with the seal boy. Could this strange weave of seaweed really be his? It did not appear as if the seaweed had been haphazardly thrown together by the waves; rather it seemed as if they had been purposefully fastened together, one to the other, to form a kind of garment. When Elsie shook them, they did not fall asunder, which they would surely have done had their union been accidental. The photograph, the patch of cloth on the injured pup, the rocking of Maurice's boat and now this curious mesh of seaweed. The evidence was still very slender but it was more than enough to keep her hopes alive.

Chapter Five

Next day was a bright sunny day. It was late July and the pendulous red flowers of fuchsia still blazed on the hedgerows. Julia came down to the strand in a light yellow print dress and cardigan and set about sketching the seals, as she had been urged to do.

'You must not expect too much,' she insisted to Elsie, 'my first efforts will be less than perfect. It will take me some time to get used to the feel of the pencil in my hand again.'

'Do you like Mr Harold? Malcolm, I mean?' Elsie asked with typical abruptness, as her aunt focused her gaze on the seals in the water.

'Of course I like him. Why? Have you some fault to find with him?' Julia retorted, somewhat startled by the question.

'Oh no,' Elsie assured her grinning, 'but I mean, do you *really* like him?'

'Oh Elsie, please don't start imagining things,' Julia replied, though there was something less than conviction in her tone. 'Yes, Malcolm is a very nice man and yes, I like him. But that's all there is to it.'

Elsie did not press the matter further, but smiled coyly to herself.

'And you can stop that grinning, too. Just because I agreed to draw a few sketches for him doesn't mean I'm going to marry him, does it?'

Who mentioned marriage? Elsie mused. Not me.

~

Some time later they were joined by Malcolm.

'We've all been invited to the big house again,' he said. 'I've had a phone call from Miss King and apparently she has something interesting to show us.'

Julia started to gather up her gear.

'No, don't stop. There's no hurry. We'll wait until you're finished your sketch,' Malcolm intervened. 'The work of a great artist should never be interrupted,' he added good-humouredly.

Elsie walked along the strand with him and told him about her find of the woven seaweed.

'I really think that the seal boy does exist,' she admitted. 'It's possible that he might have grown acclimatised to the watery way of life, if that's all he knew. I've thought long and hard about this. His digestive system could survive raw fish if it was introduced gradually. Maybe as he grew older, he might have found the means to cook the fish.'

'Do you know anything about the baby's background?' Malcolm asked.

'I know that his mother had some form of epilepsy, but I never thought of asking — now that you mention it, it could be important.'

'Perhaps Miss King will be able to tell you something,' the man suggested. 'The couple came to visit relatives here, didn't they?'

Elsie nodded.

'It would be a bit insensitive to query the relatives, though it would be interesting to know something about the child's family —' she trailed off.

'I'd say Miss King is your best chance of information. Why don't you ask her?'

Elsie liked Malcolm. He didn't dismiss her thoughts about the seal boy as idle foolishness, nor did he half-listen as so many adults did. He treated her ideas with respect and discussed them with her, whether they were plausible or not. Paul was another who listened to her.

~

Miss King greeted them in the great entrance hall. The tick of the grandfather clock reverberated boldly through the stillness.

'I hope I have not taken you away from something more pressing,' she said, 'but my cleaning lady — she's more of a friend really — reminded me of something which might be quite significant. Did I mention the bottle of wine that is supposed to have come from the *Ellen Maria*? It's still down in the cellars.'

55

Malcolm's eyes widened in disbelief.

'A bottle of wine survived the shipwreck?'

'Yes, it did,' Miss King assured him, delighted with his enthusiasm. 'One and one only, and that's why it is so very precious.'

Apparently, quite a lot of goods had survived and floated in-shore. The wine was mainly in casks. Her ancestors had systematically drunk their way through the casks, celebrating their triumphs and bemoaning their sorrows. But this one bottle had never been breached.

'Follow me,' Miss King said, and she led the way to the cellars at the back of the house.

They reached an old green door, which creaked on its hinges when she inserted the key in the lock and turned it gently. She turned on an ancient light. The bulb flickered ominously, sparked for a moment, and then settled. Though the light was feeble and paltry, it was enough to reveal a spiralling stone stairway, leading downwards to rows of timber wine racks.

Elsie's nostrils twitched. The atmosphere was stuffy and stale.

Miss King showed no hesitation about the precise location of the precious bottle and led them towards it.

Gingerly she lifted the bottle from its resting place and dusted it lightly with a hankie.

'Here, you hold it,' she said to Malcolm.

'I'd rather not. If there is an accident, I don't want to be responsible.'

While Miss King held it, Elsie studied the bottle closely. The label was black, with a bunch of purple grapes, and the name of a French vineyard and a date in Roman numerals, also in purple.

'Wow. It's amazing to think that this very bottle was onboard the *Ellen Maria* the night of the wrecking.'

'A piece of history,' Miss King agreed. 'But there's something still more important that I have to tell you.' She paused to replace the bottle carefully on the rack. 'When the wreckers took possession of the wines and brandies, teas and tobacco that came from the ships, they brought them all here to these cellars. The cellars are all that remain of the original house, actually.'

She led them carefully back up the stone staircase, locked the door, and then continued.

'Black Annie was an astute businesswoman. She supplied goods from her stores to merchants in Kerry and Cork who weren't too fussy about how she had come by them. They were only too happy to defy the English,' she chuckled.

They followed her into the study.

'When my father was alive, Lord rest him, I remember he told me that Black Annie kept very precise records in big red ledgers of the plunder seized from each ship, and what quantity of goods was supplied to the various merchants. She didn't trust her accomplices and, not surprisingly, the records were kept very secret. The wrecking was a proper business to her, I suppose. Anyway, according to my father, the ledgers gave not only the name of the ship and the goods retrieved from each one, but also where the ship was wrecked.'

'That does sound interesting. Very interesting indeed, Miss King,' Malcolm said, excitement building in his voice, 'but do you have any idea where the ledgers might be now?'

'Well, the old house was destroyed by fire, except, obviously, the cellars,' Miss King replied. 'The cellars are rather extensive. There are quite a few store rooms. The wreckers needed space for their ill-gotten goods. I suppose the ledgers might still be down there somewhere. Most of the stores haven't been opened for years.'

'I'd love to make a search for the ledgers,' Malcolm burst in eagerly. 'If that would be all right with you?'

'Oh, yes, of course it would be quite all right,' Miss King assured him. 'However, the wiring down there is quite unsafe. I'll have to get an electrician in if you want to make a thorough search and not just a quick look around.'

Malcolm beamed in anticipation.

'That's very kind of you, Miss King. If it's not too much trouble. Though you are probably safer to have the electrics checked anyway,' he added, to justify himself. 'By the way, Elsie wants to ask you something. Go on, Elsie.'

'I hope you don't mind me asking, Miss King, but do you know anything of the family of the little boy who went missing twelve years ago, the one that apparently drowned? Did you know them?'

'Your aunt could have told you that, my dear,' she said kindly.

Elsie felt a bit foolish, though Julia didn't seem to mind in the least.

Miss King went on. 'The child's father was a fisherman, originally from Coonarone. When he got married he went to live with his wife. Somewhere in

Galway, wasn't it?' She looked to Julia for confirmation. Julia nodded.

'The child's grandfather had also been a fisherman, and possibly his father before him too. Some say that his mother had epilepsy; others insist that she had no such thing, that all that happened on that day was that she had a kind of fainting spell.'

'Thanks, Miss King,' Elsie said.

'We've taken up too much of your time already,' Julia interjected. 'I think it's time we headed for home.'

'You're more than welcome.'

They bid their adieus, and left the house, each with plenty to occupy their thoughts.

~

Elsie mulled over all she had heard in her head during the course of the day; the baby's family on his father's side had been what might fairly be called 'people of the sea', and there appeared to be more than a little doubt that his mother ever had epilepsy. Could he have survived? Really survived? But even if he had, would she ever come to meet him, for, if he did not choose to reveal himself, how could she possibly hope to find him?

~

Maurice had travelled to Tralee that morning to purchase a metal detector. It was quite expensive, but he considered it a worthwhile investment, for it would prove very useful for searching the caves.

Early evening found Maurice and Toby in the network of caves that lay in line with the cluster of rocks known as The Pirate's Bed. They brought two old-fashioned lanterns with them. Toby gazed in awe at the jagged walls of the caves.

The power of the sea, he said to himself.

His accomplice didn't notice the splendours of nature. He'd too much on his mind.

'I'll have the law on Sheehan,' Maurice vowed. 'I'll get my horse back, and soon. Mark my words, Toby, I'll get my revenge.'

Maurice's talk of 'the law' was nothing more than bravado, Toby was sure of that, but the threat of revenge was more ominous and real, for he knew how vengeful and vindictive his partner could be.

The first cave they explored was vast and gloomy. The second was quite modest by comparison. But there was nothing in either except seaweed, shells and the smell of brine. It was a pattern that was to be repeated time and again during the remainder of their search.

Maurice cursed in frustration. 'The silver is still in Coonarone. I can feel it in my bones. And when I find it, I'll put the ones who sneered at me in their place.'

When they emerged from the caves, they saw a man in a boat far out in the sea preparing to dive. It was Paul.

Maurice gritted his teeth as he clenched the metal detector in his grasp. A dark thought came to him. Divers need oxygen, but it should be quite a simple matter to tamper with one of those cylinders, or with the oxygen mask attached to it. Yes, that was how he would have his revenge for having been humiliated over the horse. Simple and effective, and who could point the finger of blame at him?

~

Elsie decided to swim with Sugra early next morning. Dawn was a very special time in Coonarone, the gold light of the sun streaming in ribbons from the edge of the eastern horizon. She had risen early a few times before, and Julia did not mind as long as she was told about it, and as long as Elsie kept her promise to swim close to the shore.

She dressed quickly and made her way silently downstairs. She collected the binoculars from the kitchen wall on her way past. She had decided to keep a record of the numbers of seals she could count at various times of the day, at dawn, in the afternoon, late in the evening, and, as the record was intended purely for herself, she'd also count them any other time she happened to be on the strand. Subconsciously, she hoped that she might catch a glimpse of the seal boy with the binoculars, though she did not translate that hope into words.

~

It was a particularly beautiful morning, the world slumbering and still. She hoped Sugra would be waiting for her. Sometimes he was and sometimes he wasn't, but it was this very lack of certainty that added to her sense of anticipation. Even if he were not there to greet her, there would always be a few of his friends swimming lazily about.

She wondered why he had chosen to take a special interest in her when the others merely regarded her with curiosity at best. She had learned from her observations that, though at first they appeared quite gregarious and sociable, the seals did in fact squabble a great deal over space on the rocks. Julia had told her that they were even more cantankerous during the moulting and breeding seasons. There was only one conclusion; Sugra, despite his enormous size, must be quite a young animal and therefore more playful.

When Elsie at last reached the strand, two of the young grey seals were playing chase in and out of the sun-sprinkled water, splashing and rolling, and mock biting each other in their exuberance. Elsie remained perfectly still, because she didn't want to disturb them.

She was fascinated by the youngsters at play. They were so full of life and energy and wild high spirits. Now she could readily appreciate why some of the older people regarded them as creatures of enchantment. A great black cormorant stood on a rock with outstretched wings, unperturbed by the seals.

When the young seals had finished their games, Elsie was suddenly distracted by the sound of violent thrashing in the water some distance out. She struggled to focus the binoculars on the source of the splashing. One of the seals, a big grey, had become entangled in one of Maurice's nets. She looked about her in despair. If it were not released in a matter of moments, it might drown.

She hesitated. What should she do? She felt so torn. She had given Julia her solemn promise that she would swim close to the shore. But she could not simply stand idly by and allow the trapped seal to drown. On impulse she pulled off her shoes and socks and doffed her dress.

The water was icy. She gasped and shivered, but rapidly adjusted. Straining every sinew, every fibre of her being, she swam towards the trapped seal. It was still struggling vainly to be free of the net, throwing up great swirls of spray and splashes. She just had to reach him in time, she told herself grimly as she stretched her arms and legs to the limit and pushed forward with all her power. Each vigorous stroke took her further and further from the shore, and nearer to the seal. Apprehension mounted. What if she couldn't disentangle the net? Should she have gone for help? But then, who could she have found at such an early hour. Despite her doubts, she knew there was no turning back now.

At last she reached the massive bull. She gasped for breath, for she had never swam so swiftly in her life. Could she release him in time? She struggled desperately with the net, but it seemed hopelessly entangled. She must set him free, she must, she told herself with mounting desperation. The net was made of tough synthetic yarn, and it seemed to cut through her flesh as she tried to wrench the tangled strands apart.

What would happen if Maurice came along?

What about Julia?

At regular intervals, the huge bulk of the seal remained perfectly still for a moment or two, but then it began to splash and thrash the water again, making frantic efforts to be free. The more frenzied the struggle, the more deeply it became ensnared in the deadly fibres.

Suddenly Elsie noticed something which filled her with despair. The seal's head was stuck in a hole in the net, and it was trying to back out, but the collar of fibres held him firm. He could not bite her, she assured herself, if she came from behind and tried to wrench the meshes apart. She knew that once his head was free, he could make his escape. And she knew that she couldn't simply swim back to the shore and abandon him to his fate.

She came closer to him. He struggled more violently, blinding her eyes with the spray he churned up. Her heart drummed with alarming intensity. If only she had a knife, it would be so much easier. She could just reach the fibres on either side of his neck. The seal lay quiet and still. Perhaps he sensed that the newcomer did not pose a threat to him. The meshes seemed stubbornly resistant but, at last, one of them about the captive's neck gave way. Then a second mesh tore apart, then a third. She could now see how deeply the netting had sunk into his neck. It cut into her fingers, hindering her efforts.

Desperation made her strong. A few more moments and the seal would be free.

Without warning, the seal lashed at her with its massive hind quarters. The impact sent her reeling, and she plummeted down, down, down, into the murky depths.

Chapter Six

Elsie, her senses numbed by the cold and voluminous wash of water, flailed around in despair. The water became darker and even colder, flooding her, choking her. Then everything went blurry, hazy, and there were only dark shadows. She was going to drown.

Her mind drifted, giving in.

Suddenly a hand came from nowhere and grabbed her by the waist, hauling her up, up from the watery grave to the sunlit brightness of blue and gold.

It must be a dream. They say this happens when drowning. A half-naked boy with deep dark eyes and long dark hair. Skin the colour of light bronze. It was a lovely dream.

But the grip of his arms around her waist was real. She so wanted to believe in him, that her mind was playing tricks. Yet here he was. He sliced upwards through the water at incredible speed, drawing her with him. He had all the agility and grace of a seal. He was real. He was not the creation of her fanciful brain.

As they broke the surface, she spluttered and coughed, clearing out her lungs. And there he was. The seal boy. Many times she had imagined how she would meet him, but never like this.

He had risked discovery and come to save her when he might have let her drown. Maybe he had been impressed by her concern for the safety of his friend. Perhaps he had secretly watched her over the past few weeks, seen her swimming with the seals and observed her fondness for them. Had he noted how much Sugra seemed to enjoy her company?

In a matter of seconds, he came to the strand and laid her gently amongst the rocks. She gazed at him, taking everything in. His hair was dark and dripping, hanging loose about his shoulders. His dark eyes were deep and soulful, yet with something of the warmth and softness of a seal's eyes. He wore a necklet of shells about his neck, his lower body draped with seaweed. He stood before her for one split second, and then he plunged back into the water and was gone.

~

Julia was horrified when she heard of Elsie's close encounter with death.

'How could you be so foolish as to risk your life for a seal? How could you be so infantile as to make up a story about being rescued by the seal boy? What would your mother have said if I had to tell her that

66

you'd drowned because of some silly little girl's obsession with those damned seals?' she demanded angrily. 'While you are under my roof, you'll do as I say, Miss.'

Elsie had anticipated that her aunt would not be pleased when she heard what had happened, but she had not expected this degree of tongue-lashing.

'And you gave me your solemn word that you'd stay close to the shore. I've a good mind to pack your bags and shunt you off home on the next train.'

'I didn't plan to swim that far out. It was just, when I saw the seal trapped in the net ...' Elsie pleaded.

'What you did or didn't plan to do doesn't make the slightest bit of difference,' Julia countered. 'What matters is that you deliberately broke your promise and swam far out.'

Elsie was gloomy and downcast. She did not want to make Julia angry, or to get into trouble with her mother, but it seemed futile to argue with her aunt when she was in this mood.

Julia lifted an aluminium bucket containing meal for the hens, ducks and geese, and poured in some water from the kettle. As she was going out the door, she turned.

'If you want to stay on here for the rest of your holidays, you are not to go into the water again until I say you can. Is that clear?' she asked.

Elsie nodded in silence.

~

Elsie spent much of the day in her bedroom and though she felt sad at Julia's bitterness towards her, she would never forget the moment she had first set eyes on the seal boy of Coonarone. It had been a moment of the deepest magic. The horror of drowning had suddenly turned to wonder and elation. She did not know if he could speak, but she knew that he could feel and feel deeply. That was why he had come to her rescue. She wondered if he had played with the seals when he was younger. Maybe he even played with them still, for they had surely accepted him as one of their own. Had he splashed and frolicked about in the water as she had seen the two youngsters do early that morning, before the drama? She was confident that he had released the trapped seal from his prison of meshes by now, for he had probably just been about to do so when she had intervened.

The more she thought about it, the more she realised how much seals seemed to have in common with humans. They were warm-blooded, air-breathing mammals, but they had flourished in the water, whereas man had flourished on the land. The seal boy had chosen to reveal himself to her when she had been in trouble and in need of help, but would she ever see him again? It seemed unlikely.

If she wasn't allowed back down to the sea, Sugra would probably wonder why she did not come and swim with him. The big grey seal would think that she had grown tired of him and abandoned him, when, in fact, nothing could be further from the truth.

She nodded off while lying on her bed and was woken by the sound of raised voices in the room below. Julia and Malcolm seemed to be having a quarrel, and she seemed to be the cause of it.

'You should give her some credit for telling you what happened,' she heard Malcolm say in her defence. 'And so what if she imagined the seal boy coming to her rescue? It isn't exactly a cardinal sin.'

Elsie frowned. It was plain that Malcolm did not believe that she had really been rescued by the seal boy. But then, if she herself heard the story second-hand, she would surely be sceptical too.

Julia did not seem impressed with his line of argument.

'She almost drowned, for God's sake,' she retorted angrily, 'and what she said brought back a lot of unpleasant memories for me.'

'Unpleasant memories?' Malcolm repeated, curiosity in his voice, and though Elsie could not see it, there was a bemused expression on his face.

'Oh, it was all a long time ago.' Julia was dismissive, as if she regretted what she had said.

Malcolm did not reply. He just looked at her, waiting for her to elaborate.

'I got into trouble in the water myself when I was nineteen and I was rescued too. No, not by a seal boy, but by a handsome fellow about my own age,' Elsie's aunt continued, with more than a hint of reticence. 'Looking back, I don't know if I was really in danger of drowning, but I had no such doubts way back then. I had been plucked from the jaws of death by my handsome hero, and I fell in love with him. At least I thought I did, but it was only infatuation.'

There was an unexpected tenderness in Julia's voice. Malcolm listened attentively, not interrupting, but making quiet encouraging noises.

'I suppose I was very immature. I must have been, the way I behaved, because I followed him around like a lapdog,' she said wryly. 'We got engaged, and things might have worked out if I hadn't been so possessive. In the heel of the hunt, he broke it off and made tracks for England. People said it was only an adolescent crush and I'd get over my disappointment in time, but they were wrong, very wrong.'

Julia swallowed hard and pulled herself together. She continued in a more positive voice. 'I suppose rejection is difficult to take at any age, but it can be devastating at nineteen. Oh, he was sorry, truly sorry, if he had caused me any hurt. But he said a parting of the ways would be the best thing for both of us. I tried to give the impression that I was mature enough to accept it, but inside I wished he'd left me in the water to drown.'

'Coping with broken rainbows is part of life, I suppose,' Malcolm said gently. 'They come in different guises, but we all get our fair share of them.'

'I suppose we do,' Julia mused, and then changed the subject.

~

Maurice was becoming increasingly frustrated. Toby and he had searched more and more caves, and had found absolutely nothing.

A discovery was made at Coonarone over the next few days, however.

Julia did not relent on her decree that Elsie could not go swimming again until she understood the gravity of what had happened. She did allow Elsie to go out with Paul in his boat, on the basis that she couldn't get into much trouble with him keeping an eye on her.

Paul went diving off the boat, leaving Elsie sitting quietly. She did not know it, but Maurice had his binoculars trained on her. If only that girl had not been with Sheehan, he might have tampered with his diving gear, but she seemed to be with him so often these days.

Paul swam about in the blue green swell. He had just purchased an underwater camera. It was second-hand, but as good as new, and he was anxious to try it out in these familiar waters. When he became more expert in handling it, he would swim further out to sea.

Elsie was as excited as he was. If she couldn't go diving herself, the next best thing was to view the seabed through Paul's photographs.

There were flounders and plaice in abundance all around him. This explained why the area was so attractive to the seals. It was a wonderful sensation to swim beneath the surface. It was like moving about in a different world. The environment here was totally different to that on land. There was the ever-changing colour of the light, the unexpected beauty of the rocks and stones; the splendour of the marine flora, waving gracefully in the translucent water. But most of all there was the myriad of living things, a world teeming with life in all its diversity. Paul held the camera as firmly as he could, but it was a bit unwieldy. It would take some time to grow accustomed to it. Nevertheless, he wanted his first dive with it to be something special.

Time did not drag for Elsie as she waited above him in the boat. If she could not swim with the seals, she could admire them in the distance. She did not feel any resentment towards Julia for imposing this ban. She knew that she had been very foolish and, besides, she now knew Julia's secret, which influenced her attitude. She had not broached the subject of the broken engagement with her, as she shouldn't really have been eavesdropping and didn't want to get into more trouble.

She strained her eyes to see if she could spot Sugra, but the seals were too far away and she could not distinguish one from the other.

A few minutes later, Paul surfaced. He seemed very excited as he gently handed the camera to her.

'Be careful with that,' he told her, slightly breathless. 'There's something curious lying on the seabed. There was a lobster moving around it, which attracted me to it. I couldn't bring it up, because of the camera, but I'm going to dive again. I just hope I can find it.'

Before Elsie could ask precisely what he was talking about, he had disappeared below again. She placed the camera to one side and looked about her. Now the seconds did seem to drag. She wished Paul had told her what he had stumbled on. Could it be something that might suggest stronger evidence of the existence of the seal boy? She hoped not. Otherwise the seal boy would think that she had betrayed him. In fact, she had told no one but Julia and Malcolm, and neither of them had believed her anyway, though Malcolm was sympathetic.

She moved about in the boat, causing it to sway gently from side to side. A few seagulls passed silently overhead. Paul was taking for ever. Perhaps he had merely come upon something that had been lost by a fisherman or another diver. She looked at her watch. The movement of the minute-hand seemed incredibly slow. She hoped his enthusiasm would not lead him into danger, for she could do nothing to help him if that were to happen.

It was some time later before he finally reappeared and she sighed with relief.

'What on earth took you so long?' she asked as she helped him on board.

'I think it's made of silver,' he gasped as he held forth the object he had found.

It was covered with green slimy grime, but Elsie's heart began to throb as she studied it closely.

'It looks like a silver candlestick,' she said excitedly.

'Well, we won't know for certain till we've had it cleaned,' Paul told her, 'and God knows, I'm no expert, but it looks like silver to me.'

First the seal boy, and now a candlestick that might have come from the *Ellen Maria*. Everything seemed to be happening at once.

'We'll take it to the antique shop in Killorglin as soon as we get home,' Paul suggested. 'We'll drop in and tell Julia where we're going. While the candlestick is being cleaned, we might have a look out for the common seals on the estuary of the Laune. I can't promise that we will definitely see them; sometimes they are there and sometimes they are not.'

Paul had told her about the common seals who frequented sandy estuaries. Their muzzles were shorter and more snubby than the greys, but the main identifying feature was their v-shaped nostrils. He had offered to drive her over on his motor bike to see them, but they had never quite got around to it before.

~

Julia did not object to Elsie travelling with Paul, provided she wore a helmet, and so they were soon on their way. When they reached Killorglin, they handed in their find. The owner of the antique shop was intrigued by it, and assured them that he would be more than happy to give it a preliminary clean for them. Then they headed for the estuary and Elsie smiled with delight when she saw two whiskered heads in the water. They looked pale brown in colour, sprinkled with darker spots and blotches.

'They'll soon begin to moult,' Paul told her. 'Late July and early August is the peak moulting season for common seals.'

Elsie felt happy again. The sight of the curious seals filled her with delight. And Paul shared her admiration, which added to the pleasure.

~

Maurice seemed to pass from one new fad to another in a matter of weeks, or even days, and though he had not yet given up hope of finding the silver, he had a new whim.

He had come across a bow and arrows in a junk shop in Tralee.

'Are you thinking of joining the Red Indians and moving to a reservation?' Toby laughed at him.

But Maurice had other plans. He prided himself as a marksman, and what better target than those damned seals that were forever plaguing him. He thought of the great whaling ships. He had seen them on television and when they made a kill, the brine ran red with blood.

While Paul and Elsie were admiring the seals on the river Laune, Maurice sat in his boat and focused on his first luckless victim in the waters off Coonarone. Toby was not with him. He might rock the boat, or distract him.

The bow Maurice held was no flimsy contraption, but a powerful weapon of destruction. The long shining metallic arrows glistened in the sunlight. He held the arrow in position and prepared to shoot. One shot through the head, and the seal would be dead.

The unsuspecting seal lay motionless in the water. He was 'bottling', sleeping at sea. A second later, the arrow left the bow, a shining angel of death slicing the air in two as it ripped towards its target. Though the point of impact was somewhat lower than Maurice had intended, he had hit his mark. Blood began to spew from the wound, reddening the sea all around it. Maurice grinned triumphantly.

'I still have the knack,' he gloated, 'and maybe the sight of all that blood will drive the damn seals elsewhere.'

Chapter Seven

It was difficult keeping secrets in the townland of Coonarone, and soon the area was agog with excitement at the discovery of the antique silver candlestick, for that is what it proved to be. What's more, it was probably from the *Ellen Maria*.

The local newspapers carried special features on the discovery. Paul insisted that Elsie share the limelight with him; after all, she had been with him when he had found the candlestick.

Julia organised what she called 'a little celebration' at the farm house, with the candlestick occupying pride of place on the living room table.

'The candlestick proves beyond doubt that there was silver on board the *Ellen Maria* when she was wrecked by Black Annie and her gang,' Malcolm remarked pensively as they lingered at the table after their meal. 'But it raises as many questions as it answers.'

'What kind of questions?' Julia asked, somewhat surprised.

'Well, the most important question would be, did the rest of the silver plunge to the bottom of the sea too, or did the captain bring it ashore, as local tradition suggests,' Malcolm replied. 'The candlestick is a marvellous find, but, after all these years in the salt water, it's not in the best condition. If the rest of the silver shared its fate, then it's probable that it too would be falling apart by now.'

Elsie listened intently.

'But if the silver was scattered all over the seabed, surely someone would have come across at least a few pieces by now?' Paul suggested.

'You'd think they would have,' Malcolm agreed. 'On the other hand, just think of the vast expanses of water along the coastline here and ask yourself, how many divers have gone diving in them.'

'I suppose you've got a point. Apart from me, most divers haven't even heard of Coonarone. I guess a team of divers would need to undertake a fairly thorough search before you could say for certain that the rest of the silver didn't sink too.'

'Exactly,' Malcolm went on, 'which is why it's still so important to try and locate those ledgers in the cellars at the big house. The precise location of the wrecking seems to be the key if there is to be any hope that the silver will be found again.'

Some time later, Julia took Elsie aside in the kitchen and told her she might go swimming with the seals again. Elsie's heart danced for joy, for she had missed being with her whiskered friends.

'I hope you don't think I've been too harsh with you, but I really was horrified when you told me about your close encounter with death.'

'That's okay, I understand. No grudge borne. All that matters now is that I can swim with the seals again,' Elsie glowed. 'Could, could I go down to the strand now?' she asked impulsively.

Julia nodded, smiling. 'Though you were foolish to swim out so far to help the seal, I have to admit I did many a foolish thing in my own day. Run along, get your togs. And be careful!'

~

It was late evening, but the sun still shone, burnished gold on the tide. The rain showers had cleared and the atmosphere was clammy and moist. There was one advantage, however. The water was still quite warm. There were a few whiskered heads in the water and Elsie was elated.

But where was Sugra? She hoped that he had not forgotten her. She looked about her, but there seemed to be no sign of him at all. Where could he be? Some of the seals were diving a little distance from her, their contours a fluid downward curve, and then erupting from the sea with agility, speed and grace.

Elsie felt listless and dreamy. She lay back in the water, pretending to 'bottle' like the seals. Her head was motionless, her eyes closed, and then she grinned when she thought of how silly she would look to a passer-by. She wondered idly did seals dream when they slept at sea. What sort of dreams would they have? Did they dream of grabbing the biggest salmon they had ever seen? Or feasting at will on an abundant shoal of herring or cod?

She became drowsier and started to daydream. Imagine if there were uppercrust seals, dressed in black swallow-tailed suits, starched white shirts and black bow-ties, seated in a grand dining room where they ordered all manner of fish delicacies from the waiter.

She was roused from her reverie by a gentle tap on the shoulder.

Was it the seal boy? Was it really him?

He fixed his dark watery eyes on her and, though he did not speak, she sensed that he revealed himself to her again for a purpose. He turned and began to swim parallel to the shore, keeping his head beneath the water much of the time, beckoning her to follow. She did not hesitate.

Where was he leading her? What did he want her to do? Her head was full of questions, but she had no answers. She'd just have to wait and see.

Sometimes his presence in the water was only betrayed by the gentle splash of water behind him. It was no great wonder that he had escaped detection for so long. How his mother would love to see him again, if she knew he was alive, but would she recognise him as her son? The seal boy sensed that his companion was not nearly as expert in the water as he, and he slowed down to match her pace.

After some time, he came to a halt and emerged onto the strand. Elsie did likewise and followed him across the craggy rocks. She recognised where she was. This was the breeding area Paul had told her about.

The rocks were sharp and jagged, but the seal boy trod on them entirely unperturbed. The soles of his feet were probably hardened by long exposure to the elements. Elsie, however, moved much more cautiously, trying to avoid the more painful edges.

When he came to the entrance to the caves, he stood and waited for her to come close. Suddenly, abruptly, he reached out his hand and took hers in his, as if to reassure her that no danger lay within. The sensation was incredibly strange, for his skin did not feel like human skin at all. It was so smooth and tough, it might have been the skin of a wild sea creature.

The tunnel that gave access to the caves was dark and gloomy, but Elsie could just about discern the dripping walls of cold stone.

Where is he taking me, she wondered with some apprehension. She could not stay too long, for she had promised Julia that she wouldn't delay.

The seal boy led her onwards, through a maze of caves, some big, some small.

If he abandons me, she thought, I'll never ever find my way out.

At last he came to a cave set deep in the base of the cliff. To Elsie's surprise, it was perfectly dry, as if the sea hadn't visited it for years and years.

Elsie gasped in dismay. A huge grey seal lay with a gaping wound in its lower neck. The wound was deep and raw. In the gloom, Elsie could not be sure if it was Sugra or not. The seal boy stooped over the injured seal, stroking it with such tenderness that she was filled with wonder. His caresses were so sensitive and reassuring that the big grey seemed comforted by his presence.

The boy beckoned to Elsie to come closer. She hesitated briefly for, though the seal seemed relaxed and unthreatened, she remembered what Paul had told her of the sharpness and swiftness of their bite.

The seal boy gazed at her intently, as if willing her towards him, and when she moved slowly across, he took her hand in his again and stroked the seal with it. At first she shivered with fright, but her fears dissipated and she revelled in the moment.

The seal seemed incredibly gentle and trusting, yet its wildness was undiminished. This was something Elsie would never forget, a moment she would savour all her life. The seal's coat was so sleek. She was relieved to find, close up, that it wasn't Sugra. Not that she wanted any seal to be injured like this.

The seal boy distracted her, an urgency in his eyes. The seal needed help, and soon, if it was to survive.

'Can I bring my friend Paul?' Elsie asked. 'He'll know what to do.'

The seal boy looked at her curiously, but made no answer.

'He's a student vet, and he's very fond of seals. You can keep out of sight while he's here, as long as you leave some kind of trail for me to follow when I come back to the entrance.'

Elsie was not sure if he understood what she said, but he nodded agreement.

'And tell your friend the seal about him, so that she knows he's only coming to help her,' the girl added as an afterthought.

Then the seal boy hurriedly led the way back through the caves and to the rapidly fading sunlight.

~

Elsie couldn't do anything until the next afternoon. Julia kept her busy about the house all morning. Elsie became more frantic as the day wore on. She had to get help for the seal and fast.

At last, Julia told her she'd done enough housework for one day, and that she could have the rest of the day off.

'Thanks, Auntie Julia. Bye. I'm off down to the beach. See you later.'

She cycled there as fast as she could.

~

She was in luck. She came upon Paul making ready to push out his boat to go for another dive. She quickly told him about the injured seal she had 'found' and even about how she had stroked it.

'You must come and treat the wound. Now. Otherwise it will fester and the seal will die. Please?' she pleaded.

Paul was impressed with her concern, but he looked at her with more than a little incredulity.

'Did it really allow you to stroke it?'

'Yes, yes, it did,' Elsie assured him.

'There's no harm in having a look,' Paul concluded, 'but I'm not sure if I can really do anything to help. I'll go back to the house and fetch my bag. I'll only be a few minutes. Wait here.'

~

Those few minutes seemed to the longest Elsie had ever known. Her anxiety to help the wounded seal made her more and more impatient with each passing second.

But how had the seal been wounded? The gash appeared too deep to have been caused by a close encounter with one of the many jagged rocks both above and below the surface of the water. Besides, the seals were intimately acquainted with such hazards and were careful to avoid them. The more she thought about it, the more Maurice seemed like the villain of the piece. Yet the wound did not appear to have been caused by a bullet.

Paul arrived back at last and they headed for the caves.

'What were you doing in the caves in the first place?' Paul asked, curious.

'Just looking around,' she told him vaguely.

'If you really stroked the seal, you were very lucky to escape with your hand intact,' he said.

But then Paul didn't understand fully, and she couldn't tell him.

They moved with increasing urgency and, in a matter of moments, the entrance loomed before them. Beyond it lay a trail of periwinkle shells left by the seal boy.

'I ... I left a trail so that I could find my way back,' she stammered.

'A clever idea,' he complimented. 'I'd never have thought of that.'

~

They reached the wounded seal at last and Paul grimaced in disgust. The wound was messy and raw. The seal made no attempt to struggle away, which Paul thought very strange indeed. Even in its present weakened condition, he thought it would make some effort to escape.

'Don't get too close, Elsie,' he urged, 'it might be more unpredictable than you imagine. Look at those ferocious teeth.'

Next moment he gaped in bewilderment as he saw Elsie stoop low and gently stroke it. The seal did not seem perturbed in the least. On the contrary, it seemed to welcome her attentions. This encouraged Paul to come closer too and he was soon dealing with the wound. He dabbed it with disinfectant, smeared some soothing yellow ointment around it and applied a piece of soft gauze to protect the rawness and soreness.

'The gauze will let the wound breathe,' he explained. 'I'm a firm believer in the healing powers of nature. Sometimes more harm than good is done by too much intervention.'

He felt elated when he had finished, as he returned the ointment to his bag.

'It's been some week,' he told Elsie as they sat with the seal a little while, stroking it, and Elsie murmured gently, soothingly.

~

At that very minute, Maurice and Toby were engaged in a bitter quarrel. The latter was enraged at what he believed to be Maurice's slaughter of the seal, for Maurice had told him boastfully that he had shot the seal and that it sank to the bottom the moment the arrow struck its head.

'Why did you do that, you eejit?' Toby demanded. 'Don't you know it's back luck to kill a seal?'

'Bad luck, my elbow. That's nothing but *piseogs*,' Maurice said dismissively.

'Now that's very easy for you to say, isn't it, Maurice? You were always a man for the easy way out,' Toby countered. 'But the old people swear that the man that kills a seal never has a day's luck afterwards.'

Maurice paused to light a cigarette and then blew impudent smoke rings into Toby's face. Resentment smouldered in his eyes.

'Yeah, and they tell stories of seals giving people rides on their backs when they are in a hurry to the fair,' Maurice snorted. 'And when they get to the far strand, the seal becomes a man and drinks a pint in the pub with the best of them before strolling out the door and never being seen again.'

He took another drag of his cigarette. 'Oh, will you leave me alone with your old yarns. Those days are dead and buried,' he concluded.

'All right, they do make up stories,' Toby admitted. But he wasn't ceding defeat. 'You've a very short memory if you can't remember how Tim Crowley fared after he shot that seal.'

Maurice knew well enough of Tim Crowley's fate, and he didn't want to be reminded of it now. But Toby insisted on telling him.

'His cattle died, left, right and centre, and the vet couldn't make head nor tail of it, even though he carried out tests to beat the band.'

'Ah, that was thirty years ago, Toby. You were only four years old then and, besides, they hadn't a clue about diseases in those days.' Maurice was as dismissive as ever.

'Well, I wouldn't be too sure,' Toby said doubtfully. 'Anyway, you can count me out of your schemes from now on.'

Suddenly Maurice grabbed him by the collar and eyed him coldly, teeth gritted.

'You're afraid of your own shadow, Toby,' he spat. 'You have the spine of a weasel. I'm better off without you.'

'And I'm better off without you!' Toby snapped back. He was tired of being intimidated by Maurice and his kind. 'I'm getting a part-time job in the garage in the village. I don't need your kind of work.'

'Off with you, then, and get yourself plastered with grease and oil, for you deserve no better,' Maurice retorted, pushing him away in disgust.

Toby left the yard in silence and he felt a curious sense of relief that he had parted company with Maurice.

'And don't come crawling back to me when I find the silver!' Maurice hurled after him.

~

Maurice drove down to the strand. Elsie and Paul were nowhere to be seen. There was Paul's boat, close to the shore, his diving gear on board. Maurice waded out, withdrew a knife from his pocket and made a slit in the tube that fed the oxygen from the cylinder to the face-mask.

'I'll show that snivelling Toby who's afraid of bad luck,' he muttered.

For good measure, he tampered with the valve that regulated the diver's supply of oxygen.

~

Paul was undecided about whether to proceed with his dive after all. It was getting late, but the sea was bright and calm, and very inviting.

He fitted on his wet suit and headed across the bay in the boat. Elsie stood on the shore, watching him go. She wished she could go too, but knew her aunt would be wondering where she was.

Some time later, Paul tumbled backwards into the clear green water. The sea closed gently over him. He looked about him in anticipation, but suddenly realised that something was amiss.

There wasn't enough oxygen getting through. He gasped for breath. Brine, not oxygen, flooded his mouth, for the pressure of the sea water had forced open the slit in the tube, flooding into the breach.

He struggled wildly, legs and arms thrashing. His heart drummed with alarming intensity. He tried to scream, but his screams were smothered by the sea that pressed in on him.

Chapter Eight

As Elsie crested the hill on her way home, she turned back for a last look at the sea. She gasped in horror. Paul's boat was overturned. Something must be wrong. She glanced around, in despair, and spotted Malcolm coming towards her in his car. She hailed him agitatedly and pointed to the upturned boat.

'Something's wrong. Paul is out there, diving, but his boat — we've got to do something.'

In seconds, she had joined him in the car and they were speeding back to the strand. There were always a few fishing boats bobbing up and down in the water.

They commandeered one, Malcolm switching on the outboard motor.

Elsie clenched her fingers unconsciously. They had to be on time. Had to be.

Malcolm's expression was strained and tense as the prow of the small vessel sliced through the water.

'I don't understand how the boat could overturn. The sea is so calm,' Malcolm said, puzzled. But Elsie sensed that the seal boy was trying to signal to her that her friend was in distress.

As they approached the upturned boat, Malcolm quickly stripped and dived into the water, leaving the rudder in Elsie's hands.

Elsie peered, trying to see through the water, trying to follow Malcolm's descent. Every second was vital.

'Oh God,' she thought. 'It's all my fault. If I hadn't persuaded him to see the wounded seal, maybe this wouldn't have happened.' Her thoughts weren't logical, but she couldn't see that.

At that very moment, Malcolm grabbed the stricken diver and lifted him to the surface.

Paul was deathly pale and unconscious. Malcolm laid him gently in the boat, and clambered in after him. He quickly removed the mask, arranged him in the recovery position, and started massaging his chest rhythmically.

'Come on, Paul. Help me. Fight it. Breathe. Please breathe. You can do it. BREATHE!' Malcolm worked harder, pumping Paul's chest up and down, forcing the water out, making room for air.

Paul moaned gently and then started coughing, racking coughs to clear his drowning lungs.

Malcolm stopped long enough to take Paul's pulse.

'It's okay,' Malcolm told a relieved Elsie, 'he's going to be fine. But we'd better get him to the doctor for a check-up, just to be sure.'

And they headed back to shore, Paul's colour slowly returning as air filled his lungs.

~

Paul was given the all-clear by the doctor, who recommended that he spend some time in bed, resting, to help his body recover from the ordeal.

The next day Elsie called to see him. As he lay in bed, he recalled the shadow that seemed to hover about him in the water.

'I'm not a very religious person,' he told Elsie, 'and I'm not sure that I believe in guardian angels, but I felt a presence close by, as if someone was trying to see that I came to no harm.'

'You did something good for the seals, and maybe they protected you in return,' Elsie said, smiling. 'By the way, a group of divers has arrived from Dublin. They read about your find and they're going to conduct their own search for a few days.' She added, gloomily, 'All they seem to be interested in is the price the silver might fetch on the open market.'

Secretly she was dismayed, mainly because the presence of strangers would surely mean that she wouldn't meet the seal boy again. Not until they were gone, anyway. And she could not visit the caves again for the time being, in case she attracted too much attention to them.

~

But early next morning, to her surprise, the seal boy joined her as she swam. She swam alongside him and he led her to a tiny secluded inlet, some distance from the breeding caves.

The coastline was heavily indented, with many inlets, but the seal boy seemed familiar with them all. The two of them remained in the water for a little while, his eyes curious and wondering. It was obvious that he was as fascinated by her as she was by him.

He seemed in cheerful mood; perhaps the condition of the wounded seal had improved.

Elsie was elated that he had chosen to reveal himself to her again, apparently for no other reason than to be with her. It was as if he knew that, if she was going to betray him, she would have done so by now.

She wished he could speak, for she had so many questions to ask him. How had he survived, when everyone had given him up for dead? How come he made his home amongst the seals?

On the other hand, the fact that he could not communicate with words added to the mystery and mystique that surrounded him.

It was pure magic that he trusted her. And she wouldn't break that trust.

~

'Wow!' Elsie was speechless. A great band of seals gathered round him, jostling to get close to him. Elsie had been in the water with the seals many times, but they had always kept their distance, except for Sugra. Yet here they were, swimming playfully about him, coming closer for a gentle caress, then darting away through the waves. The seal boy knew them all, from the boisterous and bold to the timid and shy. The latter received a special welcome, as if to reassure them that they were as important as their more exuberant counterparts. The most marvellous part was that he did not need to coax or cajole them. The bond between the boy and the seals was almost tangible, a bond fostered and nourished over years.

Suddenly he mounted the back of a big bull seal, its enormous body smooth and streamlined. The bull then swept through the water, the seal boy astride it.

Elsie could scarcely believe her eyes. A boy riding on the back of a wild seal! Not just any boy, but a boy as wild and as graceful as the seals themselves. It was clear that this wasn't his first time, for there was not the slightest hint of awkwardness or fear in his movements.

How can he maintain his balance? she wondered in awe, for his hands didn't seem to grip the seal at all. It was like a horse and rider, a perfect union, such was the empathy and rapport between them. They were like poetry and music and dance all fused into one, and Elsie was thrilled that she was the lucky one to witness this elemental scene.

When the big grey seal came to a halt at last, the seal boy dismounted and came to Elsie's side once more. She sensed that he had ridden the seal to please her, to make her happy, and when she smiled, he smiled too.

In the past, when she tried to imagine how he lived, if he lived, she always pictured him as being lonely and desolate in the grey bleakness of the sea. But how could he be lonely with so many friends about him?

Elsie and the seal boy swam about in the water for a little while more, Elsie rejoicing in her new-found friendship.

Gosh, she thought as she waved goodbye to him, I'll have to be careful not to betray him unwittingly. If he is discovered, he'll be pursued and plagued by reporters and media people. This is his home. This is where he belongs. His life is based on a simple creed of equality and respect between him and his marine friends. When the reporters were finished with him, the scientists would descend on him, prodding and poking him, maybe even taking him away from here to some laboratory. I don't think he'd survive that.

~

Later that afternoon, Elsie, Julia and Malcolm headed up to the big house. Elsie skipped on ahead, but not so far ahead that she didn't hear their conversation.

'My wife died a few years ago,' Malcolm confided in Julia, 'and though I don't believe I could ever love another, I've come to regard you as a very special friend.'

'I think friendship is wonderful, though often underrated,' Julia replied, 'and I hope that we continue to be friends for a very long time.'

Elsie was somewhat disappointed, for she had hoped that a romance might blossom between the two of them. She knew that Julia had become very independent over the years, and probably wasn't the easiest person in the world to live with.

~

Miss King had had the wiring in the main cellar replaced, and after an extensive search, the keys for the stores were eventually found.

'The main cellar is the only one that has been in use for ... oh I don't know how long,' Miss King explained, 'so the electricity has only been installed there. We'd better bring torches with us. Better still, I have a lantern. I'll just get it.' Miss King hurried along to the kitchen and returned bearing an antiquated but functional lantern.

Elsie grimaced in disgust when she saw the heavy dark draperies of cobwebs hanging from the ceilings and walls of the old stone chambers. She tried to imagine what the scene was like two centuries before, when the wreckers brought their grim plunder up from the strand: the trundle of heavy cart wheels across stony muddied tracks, the rhythmic muffled clatter of the horses' hooves. Casks of wine and brandy lashed in place. The fuss and the flurry as the goods were unloaded and stored as quickly as possible. Black Annie, in period dress, keeping her minions in check with harsh words and haughty mien.

Though they contained no wine or brandy, the stores were not entirely empty. The searchers came upon lengths of wood, years old, that might well have been salvaged from the doomed vessels; fragments of cloth that crumbled the moment they touched them. There were wooden boxes and when Elsie touched them, shivers coursed down her spine. These boxes had surely been carried in the hands of the wreckers, hands smeared with the blood of their victims.

Malcolm and Julia were as intrigued as Elsie with their explorations, and there was great excitement when Malcolm discovered what appeared to be the remnants of a ship's quadrant.

It consisted of a graduated arc of ninety degrees and a movable arm. According to Malcolm, the sighting mechanism which should have been attached to the arm was missing.

'What was it used for?' Elsie wondered.

'Very simply, the quadrant was used to measure the altitude of the stars, both by astronomers and those at sea,' Malcolm explained. 'If we don't find the ledgers, at least we've found something of interest,' he added with a smile.

They moved from one store to the next, but their efforts to find the ledgers proved to be in vain. They had searched what appeared to be the last chamber, and Julia and Malcolm were about to concede defeat, when Elsie noticed what appeared to be the outline of a doorway, but it was all bricked up.

'Yes,' Malcolm agreed excitedly, 'it certainly looks like a doorway. But we'll have to ask Miss King's permission before we try to remove any bricks to see what lies beyond it.'

Miss King was as eager as they were to unlock the secret of the doorway, and, in a matter of moments, they set to work with a nail-file from Julia's handbag, trying to ease out the crumbling mortar.

'Better be careful not to remove too many bricks,' Malcolm cautioned, 'just enough to let Elsie scramble through, for the moment. Otherwise, the whole cellar could collapse around our ears.'

The task seemed painstakingly slow, and Miss King hummed with excitement. She wasn't too old to enjoy a bit of adventure.

At last, Malcolm deemed the opening to be large enough.

'What if there are rats?' Elsie asked, suddenly panicking.

'Don't worry, Elsie, there won't be. And anyway if there are, we're here,' Malcolm replied cheerfully.

~

Elsie edged carefully through the hole they had made, and, looking around, held the lamp aloft.

'It's a tunnel, not another chamber,' she called back to the others. 'I'll walk along it a little way to see where it goes.'

'Careful,' cautioned Julia.

She hadn't gone very far when the tunnel opened out into a small room. Elsie gasped in disbelief. There was a small oak writing desk and chair. The chair seemed ready to fall apart. She carefully placed the lantern on top of the desk, the flickering light throwing eerie shadows all around. She gingerly tugged at one of the drawers. It was reluctant to open. She tried a little harder and it suddenly flew open, and she fell back to the ground, clutching an empty drawer.

She picked herself up and was more cautious as she tried the second drawer. This time, she eased it gently and, yes, there they were. Black Annie's secret ledgers. She lifted them gently from their resting place. The spines were frayed and worn. The pages were yellowed and blotched and musty, but their secrets were intact. Carefully she stacked them in her left hand and retrieved the lantern. She glanced around her once more. There were rotting timbers thrown in a pile in a corner, an empty wooden frame hanging forlornly on the facing wall, and a sconce for holding candles. That was it. Nothing else in this subterranean room.

Elsie lingered a few moments longer. This had been Black Annie's secret place. Perhaps she held clandestine meetings with her inner circle here. Or perhaps it had been off limits to everyone but herself. It was strangely chilling to picture her at her desk, dipping her quill in the ink and dispassionately noting down the contents of the most recent haul. What strength of character she must have had to control a band of men as reckless and as ruthless as herself. Did she ever feel sympathy or compassion for her victims and their loved ones? Or had she become hardened to the destruction and slaughter? Elsie knew that not all the sailors drowned, that those who survived were murdered, so that they couldn't point an accusing finger at Annie and her evil band.

'Elsie? Elsie, are you all right? You're in there a long time. Can you hear me?' Julia was beginning to get worried.

'I'm fine. I'll be back in a minute. And wait till you see what I found.' Elsie couldn't keep the glow out of her voice.

~

Some time later, after much turning of the musty pages in the drawing room, they came at last upon a footnote which, though brief, was very dramatic.

'These [referring to casks of wine and chests of tea] taken from the *Ellen Maria* that did break up on the rocks beyond the place where the sea creatures do make their nests in caverns.'

'The place where the sea creatures do make their nests ...' Elsie repeated, with mounting excitement. This was obviously a reference to the breeding site of the seals of Coonarone. Miss King produced an old map and they perused it carefully.

Directly in line with the caverns was a cluster of rocks which were indicated on the map as *Carraigeacha na h-Aimleise*, the Rocks of Misfortune.

'And aptly named too,' Miss King remarked.

'We must keep the discovery secret,' Malcolm insisted. 'We don't want hordes of treasure seekers tramping through the breeding site. It would scare the seals off, and they might abandon their familiar haunts and find new breeding grounds. That would be a tragedy for Coonarone.'

~

The divers from Dublin soon left for home, empty-handed. They had found not one single piece of silver. Elsie was glad to see them go, because she was worried that they might discover her new friend, the seal boy.

But a new danger appeared on the horizon, in the form of a smiling young woman named Audrey McGrath.

'She's an anthropologist,' Paul explained.

'What's an anthropologist?' Elsie asked.

'They study man, his origins, his physical characteristics, religious beliefs and social relationships. That sort of thing. Audrey is specially interested in social anthropology, how people relate to the other people around them.'

It transpired that the seal boy had been mentioned in passing in some of the news bulletins at the time of the discovery of the candlestick and she had become intrigued by the stories. She was coming to see Paul's curious photograph later that evening, and she wanted to hear about the 'presence' that seemed to be close at hand when he thought he was drowning.

'Oh, and Malcolm has been speaking to her, too. He told her of your claim to have been rescued by the seal boy. You must come to my house later this evening, so that Audrey can have a chat with you.'

Elsie sighed inwardly. Just when one danger had passed, another had taken its place.

Chapter Nine

Elsie did not accept Paul's invitation to come and meet the anthropologist. She was sorry, but, 'Julia wanted help with some chores'.

However, Audrey McGrath proved to be persistent. Despite all Elsie's efforts — sneaking out the back door when the newcomer came in the front way — she was eventually confronted by her on the strand.

Audrey was very charming, with short blonde hair, blue perceptive eyes, and her clothes finely tailored.

'I don't normally chase halfway across the country on a mere hunch,' she said earnestly, as she fell into step beside Elsie, 'but something prompted me to do so. Paul Sheehan and that nice Englishman told me that you are fascinated with the story of the seal boy too.'

'Oh, it's a lovely story,' Elsie admitted, as casually as possible, 'but I don't think I ever really believed it.'

'Oh didn't you?' the newcomer retorted with some surprise. 'Paul seemed to think otherwise.'

'I pretended to be really interested, because Paul was very nice to me, but he gets a bit carried away about things.' Elsie was trying to appear detached.

'And what did you make of the photograph?' Audrey persisted, eyeing her companion closely.

'I don't really know what I made of it,' Elsie replied thoughtfully, for she felt it best not to appear too negative. 'I suppose it could be a seal boy if you wanted it to be a seal boy, but it could be so many other things too.'

'That's the problem, isn't it?' Audrey agreed in her charming way.

Elsie wished she wasn't so polite and agreeable. Then she herself would not feel so guilty about deceiving her. Yet she had to protect the seal boy at all costs.

'The Englishman — Malcolm, isn't it? — he told me you claimed you'd been rescued by the seal boy,' Audrey went on.

'I made that up,' Elsie stammered, feigning embarrassment, fidgeting uncomfortably with her hands. 'I knew I'd get into trouble with my aunt when I told her I got in difficulties, so I made up the bit about the seal boy as a kind of distraction.'

'Oh? But Malcolm said that you were very convincing in your descriptions of the seal boy.'

Elsie tried to appear self-conscious.

'My imagination gets the better of me at times. I'm always daydreaming at school.'

Audrey didn't prolong the encounter much longer. She knew she had more than enough to be going on with.

'I've got to go now,' Elsie said, and raced off.

~

Audrey had had enough time to form some impressions about Elsie. She appeared to be a very pleasant girl. However, she had done her best to seem dismissive of the seal boy and the legends that surrounded him. It was almost as if she were concealing a secret. Yet what could that secret possibly be? Audrey hesitated. Was she simply reading too much into Elsie's strained expression of disinterest? Yet it would be foolish not to probe matters a little more deeply, having come all this way.

~

Julia recommended that Malcolm should not let anything slip to Audrey of their discovery of the ledgers.

'You said it yourself, Malcolm. I know that Audrey is not a treasure hunter, but she might innocently pass on the information to others less scrupulous than herself.'

It proved to be very sound advice, for Audrey soon found herself a guide, none other than the poacher, Maurice. She had heard whisperings of his poaching activities but, as far as she was concerned, so much the better. He would be more intimately familiar with the coastline and its many inlets.

Julia wondered why Elsie had so suddenly lost all interest in the seal boy. There were days when she had been able to talk of little else. She would have thought the girl would hang on Audrey's every word and be at her side every moment of the day.

Elsie's excuse was she didn't like Maurice O'Connell, especially since the morning she saw him attempting to shoot one of the seals.

Maurice thought it bizarre that Audrey should be more interested in the seal boy than in the silver. He told her all about the silver, in the hope that she might join forces with him in the search. Though he would never have admitted that he needed her help, he could see that she was a clever, resourceful woman, who might readily hit upon a scheme to locate the treasure in all its shining glory. But as long as she paid him, and paid him well, what did it matter? He would tell her all the stories he knew of the seal boy and would add a few embellishments here and there for good measure. Sure, where was the harm in making a good story better?

Audrey soon perceived his fondness for extravagant words, however, and decided to discount much of what he said, though he could be quite convincing and persuasive at times.

'It would be fascinating to run tests on a boy like the seal boy,' she mused one day, as she sat in Maurice's boat preparing to dive. The sky was gloomy and overcast, the threat of rain in the wind.

'What kinds of test?' Maurice asked.

'All kinds,' Audrey told him vaguely, suspecting that if she went into too much detail, her companion would not understand. 'You see, man is a terrestrial or land-based creature, so it would be exciting to discover what changes might occur, in his senses or his metabolism, for instance, if he spent nine-tenths of his time in the water from a very early age.'

'Hmmph!' Maurice was not unduly impressed, nor was he convinced when Audrey suggested that the discovery of the seal boy would be worth more than all the silver in the world.

She adjusted her face mask, and went overboard. Even if he did exist, it was like searching for a needle in the proverbial haystack. But, on the other hand, if she found nothing of interest, she would enjoy the dive.

Worth more than all the silver in the world, eh? Maurice grinned to himself. Maybe he could put that to the test, if the seal boy happened to stray across his path. Audrey could have him for her precious tests, but he, himself, would sell the story of the boy's capture to the highest bidder. He had read somewhere that the English papers were willing to pay five-figure sums, even six-figure sums for such stories.

Audrey's dive proved fruitless and when she and her companion came back to the strand, they found Paul making ready to push his own boat into the water.

Paul had now fully recovered from his harrowing ordeal some days earlier, and, though his mother had begged him not to go diving so soon again, he had not heeded her pleas. If he did not return to the water now, he knew that his fears would take hold of him and would prevent him from doing so ever again. He had discovered the slit in the oxygen tube attached to his mask and, though it was possible that the slit might have been caused accidentally, it had all the hallmarks of having been made with a sharp blade. And it seemed to him that there could only be one culprit: Maurice. No one else would stoop so low.

'When are you bringing my horse back, Sheehan?' Maurice demanded angrily as they approached each other. Audrey looked on with more than a little apprehension. 'And you're no better than a common thief for taking her in the first place.'

Paul did not respond at first, for he was unwilling to allow himself to be goaded. Also, he couldn't confront him about the diving gear without some proof that Maurice had tampered with it. Instead, he turned away and exchanged a few words with Audrey.

This deliberate snub irked his antagonist even more.

'I want her back, do you hear me, Sheehan?' he roared with renewed vehemence. 'I know you'd like to see me and mine trampled into the dirt, but you're not going to get rid of me that easily, boy.'

'Your horse is being treated with a lot more dignity than you ever gave her,' Paul retorted at last as he climbed into his boat.

'Oh, is it dignity that's troubling you now?' Maurice jeered. 'The only dignity the Sheehans of Coonarone ever had was the sort that money can buy. But I'm not a crawler like the rest of them. I'll not become one to suit the likes of you.'

'For a man who's not a crawler, your brain is remarkably close to the ground,' was Paul's closing remark on the subject as he activated the outboard motor. As he sped away, he was surprised at himself, and glad he got the last word in.

'Bloody snob,' Maurice concluded dourly.

Audrey thought it wisest to make no observations on the matter at all.

~

Elsie told herself that she would not go to meet the seal boy again until Audrey had packed her bags and left Coonarone. But she could not resist the temptation to do so. Early one morning, having made certain that the beach and the sea were deserted, she swam towards the inlet where he had ridden the big grey seal. Now the coastline was enveloped in a hazy mist that reduced visibility considerably, and she told herself that he would probably not come. She lingered in the water a little, looking about her impatiently, uncertainly.

She had heard Audrey tell Malcolm of the scientific tests that could be carried out on the seal boy, and the prospect sent shivers down her spine.

Soon she heard a splash in the water, and her heart danced with joy when she saw, coming towards her, not only the seal boy but a host of whiskery heads. Sugra was amongst the newcomers and he seemed to have a special welcome for Elsie.

She told the seal boy about Audrey. He must be even more wary and vigilant while Audrey remained at Coonarone and, even though he did not speak, his intelligent eyes seemed to understand.

She swam about with the seal boy and his friends for a little while and again there was a sensation of wild undiluted exhilaration. They seemed to accept that, if the seal boy trusted her, then they could trust her too.

Elsie had brought a present for her friend. She knew that he wore a necklet of shells, but she had made a wristlet for him, fashioned from a wide band of leather with thonging at each end to fasten it. She had coated one side of it with a white plaster paste and adorned it with shells while the plaster was still wet. Then she had allowed the plaster to harden and set, so that the shells were firmly embedded in it. Finally, she had applied a coat of clear varnish, to highlight the natural beauty of the shells, and also to seal the plaster against the sea-water. She took the seal boy's right hand in hers and gently fitted the wristlet about his arm, securing it with the leather thonging.

The seal boy's dark eyes shone with delight as he caressed the wristlet admiringly with his left hand. It was the first time the seal boy had ever been given a gift and he savoured the moment to the full.

Elsie did not speak, but watched his response hopefully. He seemed intrigued by the way the shells didn't move freely like the ones in his necklet.

When he lifted his gaze from the wristlet at last, he looked at her awkwardly for a moment or two. Maybe he was wishing that he could speak the way she spoke, so that he could thank her. Then suddenly he moved close, briefly hugged her tight, and backed off again, taking Elsie totally by surprise. She was astounded by this simple, uninhibited display of affection and gratitude, which moved her more deeply than mere words could have. He was fond of the seals and he hugged them. He was fond of Elsie, so he hugged her too. His simplicity of approach was touching.

Sometimes in the past, she had tried to imagine what it might be like to have a big brother. Now she began to think of the seal boy as a brother, a very special brother.

She was so happy that she had taken the time to make the wristlet for him. Though it was a very small gesture, it seemed to make a big impression on her friend. His eyes were filled with warmth and tenderness, and she wished that things would stay like this for ever and ever.

~

Julia and Malcolm made a preliminary inspection of some of the caves which served as the breeding area for the seals, in search of the treasure. There was such a honeycomb of caves.

'It might be impossible to search them all, but we'd better start searching quickly or not at all, because soon the seals will begin breeding again,' Julia remarked.

'Yes, we certainly cannot disturb them at such a vital time,' Malcolm agreed.

~

That afternoon, Malcolm selected a few of Julia's pencil sketches for the chapter of his book dealing with Coonarone.

'It looks like being a very interesting chapter,' he assured her. 'I'll be able to make reference not only to the discovery of the silver candlestick and Black Annie's "office", but also to the legends of the seal boy. I'm nearly finished and I'll be heading back to England soon, to do some research on a coastal community in Cornwall. Maybe I'm being a bit fanciful, but what a spectacular ending to the chapter it would be if the treasure of the *Ellen Maria* were found at last.'

'It would be great, right enough,' Julia replied. 'But don't hold your breath!'

'I'll miss Coonarone when I leave, and you especially, Julia.'

'I'll miss you too, but perhaps you could come again next year?'

~

Later that evening, Elsie asked Julia would she do a special sketch, just for her.

'Certainly. What had you in mind? One of the seals? Or a group of them? You've certainly spent enough time with them.'

'N-no. Actually, I was wondering if you'd do a sort of photo-fit. Could you draw a seal boy, if I describe what I think he'd look like?'

Julia looked at her askance.

'I thought you weren't interested in him any more.'

'It's just that I'd like to have something to remember my holiday by ...' Elsie mumbled uncomfortably.

'Alright, certainly. Tell me what you want.'

Elsie dictated, and Julia sketched.

'Dark eyes. And long hair. I think. I mean, if he existed, he'd have long hair, wouldn't he?' she added quickly.

'Well, how's that?' Julia asked, as she added a few seals sunning themselves in the background.

'That's wonderful! Oh, thank you, Aunt Julia. I'll always have this to remember my summer in Coonarone. Thank you!'

~

Audrey was getting dressed in the guesthouse where she was staying. Paul had invited her to dinner and she had accepted his invitation, much to Maurice's annoyance. She had assuaged his displeasure somewhat by offering him the chance to earn some extra money.

She had made some enquiries and, not surprisingly, discovered that no one had ever taken the legend of the seal boy seriously enough to mount a vigil along the coastline of Coonarone. It was difficult to say what one man in a single boat could achieve, but she had decided that she would pay Maurice a sizeable bonus if he agreed to mount just such a vigil, all through the night and into the morning.

'A vigil?' Maurice snorted, flabbergasted at the absurdity of the notion.

'Yes, a vigil. And if I'm paying you, make sure you don't try to cheat me. All night and the next morning. Mark my words, if you don't stick to your end of the bargain, I'll hear about it, and you won't get a brass farthing from me.' She went on to give him his instructions. 'Don't use the engine on the boat. Select a good vantage point, far enough out that you can keep a watchful eye on the coastline with your binoculars.'

'It's money for nothing,' Maurice had told her bluntly. 'I might as well go fishing for mermaids.'

Maybe he's right, she told herself with more than a little misgiving, but then nothing ventured, nothing gained.

She studied her reflection in the mirror, straightened her collar, adjusted her hair.

'Right, I'll do.' She left her room and went downstairs to meet Paul.

~

Audrey was intimidating in a subtle kind of way. Though Maurice had no great enthusiasm for his task, he did his best to keep awake. He had motored out into the bay, and dropped anchor where he had a broad sweep of cliff-face in his sights. He focused his binoculars on the cliffs now and then. The moon's rays shed their reluctant light, seeming to alter the cliff face with their eerie glow. Nothing to see. He couldn't even see the cliffs clearly. Was that a shadow or a cave? He couldn't be sure. The strain of peering through the dark made his eyes hurt.

'I'll just look every so often. I can't keep this up all night,' he yawned.

He woke with a fright from a fitful slumber. He felt curiously ill at ease.

'It's all bloody Toby and his talk of bad luck.'

Brave talk was all very well when the heart was invigorated by a few pints, but it was a different matter entirely to be all alone in a boat in the night. It wouldn't be so bad if he were poaching. At least he would have something to occupy his mind. But this, sitting out on the silent sea, with only the occasional creak of the boat beneath him to break the monotony, this was a different matter. Unwelcome thoughts wandered randomly through his brain, disturbing his peace.

He was tempted to chuck it in, switch the engine on and head back to the shore. As it was, he would be the butt of so many jokes when it got around that he had spent a night out looking for the seal boy.

A gentle splash in the distance. Maurice heard it, but was not unduly interested. Probably one of those ugly seals, he told himself, as he lethargically lifted the binoculars to his eyes.

His jaw dropped, and his eyes opened wide as saucers.

There he was. There really was a seal boy! He could see him, with his own two eyes.

The seal boy, unaware that he was being observed, was frolicking gently at the water's edge amongst the seals.

'Wait till Audrey hears this. I'll probably get a bonus. Not to mention the money I'll make from selling the story. Now, all I have to do is catch him.'

Chapter Ten

Maurice was deep in thought as he cleaned and oiled his rifle. He could still scarcely grasp what he had seen, but when he confided in Audrey some time later, she seemed a little sceptical.

'I hope you haven't fabricated the whole thing, just to get money out of me for another vigil,' she said disparagingly.

'I swear it's true. On my mother's grave,' he insisted.

'Okay, I'll give you the benefit of the doubt,' she said grudgingly. 'Have you told anyone else what you saw?'

He shook his head.

'Well, keep it that way,' she warned. She knew her guide's penchant for bravado. 'One further piece of advice — keep an eye on that girl Elsie, Julia's niece. I have a curious feeling that she may already have met with the seal boy.'

~

Elsie went boating with Paul later that day and, everywhere they went, Maurice's boat was never out of view. Paul felt ill at ease. Maurice was obviously shadowing them. But why? He knew that Maurice still bore a grudge over the horse — and a great many other things besides — but who could say what warped and distorted notions lurked in his hostile little brain.

Paul had intended to go for a dive, but decided against it, in view of Maurice's disconcerting interest in them.

'Maybe I'm being paranoid,' Paul told Elsie as they headed back to the beach, 'but I'm not taking any chances this time. By the way, why don't you like Audrey?'

'Who says I don't like her?' Elsie snapped defensively.

'She thinks you don't. She told me herself last night,' Paul explained.

'Maybe I could have been a bit more friendly,' Elsie admitted, 'but I'm not very keen on some of her notions. If she captured the seal boy, for instance, she'd lock him up and use him as a kind of guinea pig.'

'Well, you must admit he would be an interesting subject for a scientific study.'

'Maybe he would,' Elsie agreed doubtfully, 'but would she respect his feelings? If he lost his freedom, I think the seal boy would lose everything.'

Paul looked at Elsie closely. There was something in the intensity and passion of her tone that suggested that she really believed he existed.

'Anyway, it doesn't really matter, does it?' she added, attempting to be offhanded. 'After all, he doesn't exist.'

Paul was not entirely convinced.

~

The next morning the quiet stillness of the dawn gave no hint of the drama that was about to unfold.

Despite her apprehension, Elsie hurried along the beach for another rendezvous with the seal boy. Her holiday at Coonarone was drawing to a close, which made every moment she spent with him more and more precious. She would love to share her secret with someone, to tell them all about him and his wonderful relationship with the seals, but she dared not, lest it endanger him in any way.

It wasn't long till she reached his favourite haunt. And there he was, a great throng of seals around him. She was overjoyed to see him. When he emerged from the water, he fixed her with his steady gaze. It was as if he were trying to read her innermost thoughts. His eyes were the most expressive she had ever seen. Though he could not speak, he had learned to communicate in a different way.

He held up his arm to show her that he still wore the wristlet. It seemed to mean a great deal to him.

Then he took her by the hand and led her hurriedly along the beach. Elsie ran as fast as she could, to keep up with him. Where was he taking her to now? she wondered. Maybe to see the wounded seal.

His eyes darted left and right as he ran, constantly alert, watching.

They eventually reached the entrance that gave access to the breeding caves. While she gasped and panted from her exertions, he didn't seem breathless at all.

His movements within the cave were somewhat less hurried, his gait less cautious, but nevertheless there was still an almost palpable urgency. The path he followed was as bewildering as before. She wondered how he could make his way so surely, so confidently, when there seemed to be little or no distinguishing features to identify one cave from the next.

Why had he brought her to the caves? Could it be that one of the cows had given birth early? She knew that the peak pupping season was September to November, but there might well be early seal pups, just as there were early spring lambs. He was clearly excited about something, and she could sense it in his taut grip about her wrist.

~

For all the seal boy's caution, Maurice was following them at a safe distance, picturing with glee the capture of his victim. He would be richer than he had ever imagined. And the snobs who had humiliated him and tried to make him feel small would sing a different tune. A greedy light danced in his eyes as he gripped the gun tightly with his sweaty palms. Audrey was right; Julia Cronin's niece *did* know the seal boy. And

116

now they were walking into his trap, like flies into a web.

Unknown to the pair, Maurice had been lurking behind a rock close to the caves. Following his chat with Audrey, he had been watching Elsie's movements over a few days, and he noticed her penchant for this area. She seemed to spend an inordinate amount of time amongst the rocks, and he intended to find out why.

When he saw the pair running quickly along the strand, he slipped quietly into one of the caves before they spotted him, and now they were within his grasp. Soon, very soon, he would be on the front page of every newspaper in Ireland and England.

The seal boy paused suddenly, looking about him uncertainly. He cocked his head sideways and listened. Elsie wasn't sure if he had lost his way, or whether he was listening for something. Then he shook his head slightly, as if to say, 'It was nothing,' and continued on deeper into the cliff face.

They turned a bend into another cavern and Elsie stopped, agape. There in a corner lay an open sea-chest, its contents glittering and dazzling. Silver goblets and trays, candlesticks and cups, ewers and wine fountains shone in pristine glory, unspoiled and untouched by the ravages of the sea. It had to be the lost treasure of the *Ellen Maria*!

She bent down and lifted out first one piece, then another. She held a magnificent wine fountain with trembling hands, turning it gently to see the ornamentation which was wild, elaborate and extravagant. The lid and sides of the fountain were lavishly decorated with rock and shell motifs.

The seal boy stood by, grinning, as she gently rummaged through the contents of the chest. Elsie could hardly believe her eyes. Was all this a dream? Would she wake up soon? But the brilliant silver sheen was real, glisteningly real.

Next she picked up what looked like a knife with a jewel-encrusted handle. The long tapered blade sparkled, sharp as the day it was made. It was a beautiful piece of workmanship.

Must be a letter-opener, she thought.

Suddenly Maurice appeared from nowhere, brandishing a rifle, his eyes shining with greed. His gaze flitted from the great chest of silver to the seal boy and back. He was in luck. Two for the price of one!

'Hah!' he cried. 'What a nice surprise.'

Elsie was stunned at his sudden appearance, but had the quickness of mind to conceal the knife she was holding. With the barrel of the gun, Maurice waved Elsie and her companion away from the chest. As they edged gingerly backwards, he eased closer and closer to the chest, and withdrew a candlestick with his free hand. He groped and pawed it with his stubby fingers, his eyes never leaving his captives. Rich! Rich beyond all imagining!

Elsie shivered. Maurice was like a man obsessed. He cast fleeting glances at the shimmering treasures, his finger ominously close to the trigger. Elsie's nerves jangled. Aunt Julia had told her that the poacher was volatile at the best of times. Who could predict what he might do?

'Come here,' Maurice demanded gruffly, addressing himself to the boy.

The seal boy remained perfectly still.

Maurice repeated the command, getting impatient.

'He doesn't understand, can't you see? You have to speak to him in sign language,' Elsie said, quickly before Maurice lost the head altogether.

'Shut up, you. I'll deal with you later,' Maurice growled, and then, reluctantly putting the candlestick down, he beckoned to the seal boy.

Slowly, very slowly, he moved towards his aggressor. When he got within arm's reach, Maurice grabbed him. The poor boy stood there, utter bewilderment in his dark eyes.

Elsie winced at the roughness of Maurice's dealings with the boy. What can I do? she thought. How can I get us out of this?

And then she remembered the knife. She'd have to wait for the right moment, because if her plan backfired, she would be placing them both in even greater danger.

Maurice turned to leave the cave, pushing the seal boy in front of him.

'Don't try any funny business, missee,' he snarled at Elsie, 'or the boy will get it in the back.'

It was now or never.

Elsie hurled the dagger with all her might, and it sank deep into Maurice's right hand. He screamed with pain and staggered sideways, blood spewing from the wound as he wrenched the dagger free.

The seal boy seized the moment and made his escape.

Maurice recovered himself sufficiently to realise that his quarry was getting away, and he gave chase, running awkwardly, the gun under his arm, and his left hand attempting to staunch the blood flow. His greed imbued his limbs with an unexpected vigour.

'You'll be sorry,' he spat at Elsie over his shoulder as he ran.

If only the seal boy can get to the sea, Elsie thought. In the sea he will be safe.

She picked up the discarded bloody knife and followed at a safe distance.

The seal boy plunged headlong through the labyrinth of caves, running for his life. He didn't know what the man wanted of him, but he didn't think it wise to wait around to find out.

When he emerged in the bright sunlight, he gaped in bewilderment, for there was another human — Audrey.

He paused for one split second and then continued on into the sea, to safety.

'Come back! Come back! We don't want to harm you!' Audrey cried, but the seal boy just swam as fast as he could, with strong, vigorous strokes.

Seconds later, Maurice appeared at the entrance to the cave, panting and gasping for breath. He spotted the boy, put his rifle to his shoulder and fired a volley of shots.

Audrey ran towards Maurice, horrified.

'Maurice, stop! What do you think you're doing? You could kill the boy. Stop!'

But Maurice had lost all sense of reason. He just pushed Audrey to one side, and continued to shoot.

Elsie emerged from the cave, swept past them, and, throwing caution to the wind, dived into the water, still clutching the knife.

Maurice was beside himself with rage.

'I won't let the seal boy escape so easily. I won't let an interfering busybody stand in my way,' he muttered as he made his way to his boat which was tied up nearby. He tossed the rifle into the boat and cast off in chase.

The fugitive had already swum a considerable distance, with Elsie labouring behind. The seal boy's entire focus was on swimming as far as possible away from the man, and to safety. In other circumstances, he would have detected the ring of nets. They were part of Maurice's traps, and were constructed in such a way that the moment a creature became entangled, the nets would collapse and hold the creature firm.

Elsie was aghast when she suddenly saw her friend struggling and flailing in the poacher's net. He'll drown, she thought with horror, he'll drown if he can't get free. Or Maurice will catch him.

She forced herself to swim even faster, in a frantic attempt to save her friend, thrusting herself forwards with renewed determination.

Maurice sped past her in his boat, its prow heading directly for the terror-stricken boy. He brought the boat to a halt and, raising the rifle, he pointed the barrel at the boy in the net.

'One more trick from you, my boy, and I'll blow your brains out!' Maurice looked around, but could see no trace of Elsie. He put the rifle aside, and reached out to drag his prey on board. This catch meant that he would never again have to bow and scrape before the upstarts of Coonarone! His efforts were hindered by his injured hand, and the fact that the seal boy was struggling, squirming, wriggling desperately to be free.

Elsie had started swimming underwater, in the hope of approaching without being seen. She wished she had the skills of the seals, the lung capacity of the seal boy. The blood pounded in her ears, and she had to come up for air. She surfaced on the other side of the boat, out of sight of Maurice, gulped fresh air into her oxygen-starved lungs, and sank beneath the surface once more, gripping the handle of the dagger firmly.

She swam under the boat, and approached the net cautiously, fearful of cutting the seal boy in her frantic attempts to cut him free. She sawed away, cutting first one, two, then three of the fibres of the net.

The seal boy was splashing so much that Maurice couldn't see that his quarry was being freed from below.

Just as Maurice's stubby fingers groped to finally grasp the seal boy, there was a flurry and he vanished, free at last. Down, down the seal boy went, the water swirling and whirling.

'He's gone! He's done for now, surely.' Maurice had no hint of remorse, only regret that the seal boy had evaded him.

The seal boy broke free from the deadly spiral of his downward spin and pushed upwards with vigorous strokes once more.

As he surfaced, Maurice reached for his gun and began firing wildly, bullets whizzing haphazardly along the surface of the water. But his aim was off, and finally, all the bullets spent, he had to concede defeat.

Elsie, her mission successful, turned and made her way slowly back to the shore. Her arms were like lead, but her spirits were high.

She heard Maurice screaming vindictively at her, but she didn't care. Her friend was free.

Audrey had stood, helpless, disbelieving, on the shore while the drama was enfolding, and when Maurice finally headed back to land, she was ready for him.

'How could you? How could you be so callous and unscrupulous?' she screamed at him. 'What were you thinking of? You could have killed the boy! What good would that have done?'

He ignored her tirade and tried to distract her by changing the subject.

'I found the silver! I'm going to be rich. I found the treasure from the *Ellen Maria*,' he cried.

'Any silver you found belongs to the people of Coonarone, not to any one individual,' she told him disparagingly.

He was about to retort when the wound on his hand started gushing again. He paled at the sight of it.

'You'd better have that attended to immediately,' Audrey urged, 'or it could prove to be very, very serious.' It was the only ruse she could think of to keep him from grabbing the silver.

~

Later that afternoon, Maurice boasted to all and sundry of his amazing encounter with the seal boy. Naturally, he omitted to tell them exactly what had gone on, or of his role in the entire affair. Most of his listeners discounted Maurice's tale as another fable coined by his inventive brain.

'If you don't believe me, you can ask Audrey. She saw him too.'

One or two gullible souls took the trouble to query Audrey on the matter.

'No, no, I saw absolutely nothing,' she said, in her charming way. 'How could I have? I was nowhere near the strand. Maurice is obviously suffering from delusions.'

Later she told Elsie why she had not corroborated the poacher's version of things.

'I was appalled by his greed, his brutality. Anyway, I've come to the conclusion that it would be cruel to remove the seal boy from his habitat, no matter how interesting he might prove to be as a subject for scientific study.'

Elsie smiled with relief.

~

Maurice's supposed encounter with the seal boy was simply laughed off by all and sundry.

The whole townland had much more interesting things to discuss — Elsie's discovery of the silver. There were callers to Julia's farmhouse all day long, each wanting to hear about it from Elsie herself. And Elsie denied any involvement on the part of Maurice, or that she had seen the seal boy. It was better that way. She hoped that Maurice had learnt his lesson.

The silver hoard was retrieved from the caves, and transferred to the local barracks for safe keeping. It would remain there until experts from the National Museum came down from Dublin to evaluate it, and to decide what was best to do with it.

Everyone said that there would surely be some reward for Elsie for finding the treasure, but the only reward Elsie wanted was the knowledge that the seal boy was free.

~

Elsie spent the last days of her holiday down at the beach, amongst the rocks, hoping to meet up with the seal boy again. But he seemed to have vanished without trace. Tinged with disappointment, she could nevertheless understand his caution after all that had happened. She was thrilled to see that the injured seal had rejoined the fold, with only a scar to identify him from the others.

She confided in Paul. She knew she could trust him, and told him exactly what had happened on that horrible day. Sharing her secret with him seemed to deepen the bond of friendship that had developed between them.

Elsie did not see the seal boy again that summer until the very last day of her holidays. It was a sultry day in late August, and she went down to say goodbye to Sugra and the rest of her watery friends. She stood on the rocks, watching them lolling about in the water. She was trying to memorise everything, to keep in her heart when she went home. And suddenly, there he was. He smiled at her, and her heart lifted. He was safe. He knew she had saved him. She waved briefly and turned away, her eyes filling with tears.

She said goodbye to Julia.

'You must come back next year. It's good to have company,' Julia said.

'I will, I promise,' Elsie replied.

Would she ever see the seal boy again? Who knows? Maybe next year ...

Also by Patrick O'Sullivan
* * *

A Girl and a Dolphin

What would it be like to see a real live dolphin?
Anna finds out when an unexpected visitor swims
into her secret cove — a bottle-nosed dolphin!
As the summer slips by, their unusual friendship
grows.

But the local fishermen don't want
unwelcome guests in their waters,
and Donal's diving for sunken treasure
must remain undisturbed.

In a story full of drama and adventure,
Patrick O'Sullivan captures all the magic of
a wild creature living close to humans.

Inspired by Fungi, the Dingle dolphin.

ISBN 0 86327 426 9

Available from:
Wolfhound Press,
68 Mountjoy Square, Dublin 1.
Tel: 01 874 0354